THE VINTAGE CAPER

Peter Mayle

WINDSOR
PARAGON

First published 2010
by Quercus
This Large Print edition published 2013
by AudioGO Ltd
by arrangement with
Quercus

Hardcover   ISBN: 978 1 4713 3648 5
Softcover   ISBN: 978 1 4713 3649 2

British Library Cataloguing in Publication Data available

Printed and bound in Great Britain by
TJ International Limited

For Jon Segal,
avec un grand merci

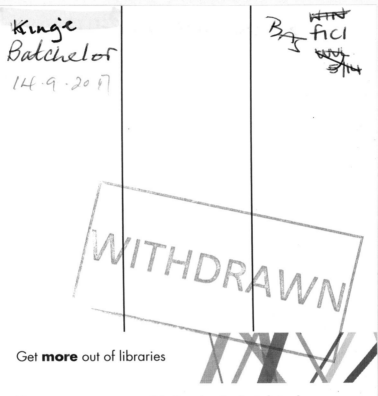

ONE

Danny Roth took a final dab of moisturizer and massaged it into his already gleaming cranium, while checking to make sure that his scalp was innocent of any trace of stubble. Some time ago, when skin had first begun to take over from hair, he had toyed with the possibilities of a ponytail, often the first refuge of the balding man. But his wife Michelle had been less than enthusiastic. "Just remember, Danny," she had said, "underneath every ponytail is a horse's ass." That had persuaded him to embrace the billiard-ball look, and he had since been gratified to find himself in the company of several stars, their bodyguards, and assorted hangers-on.

Peering into the mirror, he studied the lobe of his left ear. He was still of two minds about an earring: a dollar sign in gold, perhaps, or a platinum shark's tooth. Either would be appropriate for his profession, but were they rugged enough? Tough decision. It would have to wait.

Stepping away from the mirror, he padded into his dressing room to choose his outfit for the day, something that would take him through a morning of client meetings, lunch at the Ivy, and a private screening in the evening. Something conservative (he was, after all, a lawyer) but with a devil-may-care touch of informality — he was, after all, an entertainment lawyer.

A few minutes later, dressed in a dark-gray suit of superfine worsted, a white open-neck silk shirt, Gucci loafers, and socks of buttercup yellow, he picked up his Black-Berry from the bedside table, blew an air kiss in the general direction of his sleeping wife, and went downstairs to the granite and stainless steel splendors of the kitchen. A pot of fresh coffee and *Variety, The Hollywood Reporter,* and the *L.A. Times,* provided by the maid, had been placed on the kitchen counter. The early-morning sun was up, promising another glorious day. The world was as it should be for a member of Hollywood's professional elite.

Roth could hardly complain at the hand life had dealt him. He had a young, blond, fashionably gaunt wife; a thriving business; a pied-à-terre in New York; a ski lodge in

Aspen; and — the house that he considered his headquarters — a three-story steel-and-glass pile in the gated, high-security community of Hollywood Heights. It was here that he kept his treasures.

Like many of his contemporaries, he had accumulated a selection of socially impressive accessories. There were diamonds and closets full of status clothing for his wife; three Warhols and a Basquiat for his living room walls; a strolling Giacometti for his terrace; and a perfectly restored gull-wing Mercedes for his garage. But his favorite indulgence — and, in a sense, the cause of some frustration — was his wine collection.

It had taken many years and a great deal of money to put together what was, so Roth had been told by none other than Jean-Luc, his wine consultant, one of the best private cellars in town. Perhaps *the* best. There were the top-level Californian reds and a wide selection of the most distinguished white Burgundies. There were even three entire cases of the magnificent '75 Yquem. But the crown jewels of the collection — and the source, understandably, of great pride — were the five hundred or so bottles of *premier cru* claret from Bordeaux. Not only were they first-growth; they were also from the great vintages. The '53 Lafite Rothschild, the '61 Latour, the '83 Margaux, the '82 Figeac, the '70 Pétrus — these were stored in a cellar beneath the house and kept permanently at 56 to 58 degrees Fahrenheit, with an 80 percent humidity level. Roth added to them from time to time, when the odd case came on the market, but he seldom took any of these great bottles upstairs to drink. Just *possessing* them was enough. Or it had been, until quite recently.

Over the past few weeks, Roth's enjoyment as he contemplated the contents of his cellar had been less keen than usual. The problem was that, apart from a very few privileged souls, nobody ever saw the bottles of Latour and Margaux and Pétrus, and those who did often were not sufficiently impressed. Only last night, a visiting couple from Malibu had been given the grand tour of the cellar — three million dollars' worth of wine! — and they hadn't even bothered to remove their sunglasses. Worse still, they had then declined the Opus One served with dinner and demanded iced tea. No appreciation, no respect. It was the kind of evening that could make a serious wine collector weep.

Shaking his head at the memory, Roth paused on his way to the garage to admire the view: west to Beverly Hills, east to Thai Town and Little Armenia, south across the endless shimmering sprawl to the toy-sized planes that came and went from LAX. Perhaps not the prettiest of views, particularly when the smog was up; but it was a high view, a long view, an expensive view, and, best of all, *his* view. Mine, all mine, he sometimes thought to himself, especially at night when the lights below made a shining carpet that stretched for miles.

He squirmed his way into the snug confines of his Mercedes and inhaled the perfume of well-nourished leather and polished walnut. This particular model was one of the great classic cars, so old that it predated the invention of the beverage container, and Rafael, the Mexican caretaker, looked after it as though it were a museum piece. Roth eased it out of the garage and headed for his office on Wilshire Boulevard, his mind going back to his wine cellar and that dumb couple from Malibu, whom he'd never liked anyway.

From thinking about them, it was only a short mental hop to a more philosophical consideration of the joys of pos session. And here, Roth had to admit that the appreciation — even the envy — of others was crucial to his own enjoyment. Where, he asked himself, is the satisfaction of having desirable possessions that others hardly ever see? Why, it would be like keeping his youthful, blond wife locked away from public view, or sentencing the Mercedes to a lifetime of confinement in the garage. And yet, here he was, keeping millions of dollars' worth of the world's finest wines in a cellar that was unlikely to see more than half a dozen visitors a year.

By the time he reached the tinted-glass box that contained his office, Roth had come to two conclusions: first, that inconspicuous consumption was for wimps; and second, that his wine collection deserved a wider audience.

He stepped out of the elevator and walked toward his corner office, bracing himself for the daily *mano a mano* with his executive secretary, Cecilia Volpé. Strictly speaking, she was not quite up to the job. Her spelling was lamentable, her memory frequently patchy, and her attitude toward many of Roth's clients one of patrician disdain. But there were consolations: she had the most spectacular legs, long and permanently tanned, made even longer by a seemingly inexhaustible supply of four-inch heels. And she was the only daughter of Myron Volpé, the current head of the Volpé dynasty that had pounced upon the movie business two generations ago and that still maintained considerable influence behind the scenes. As Cecilia had been heard to say, the Volpés were the closest it got in Hollywood to a royal family.

And so Roth tolerated her for her connections, despite her lengthy personal calls, her frequent makeup breaks, and that atrocious spelling. As for Cecilia, for whom work was something to do between dates, her duties were largely decorative and ceremonial. Roth's office provided a socially acceptable base, undemanding tasks (she had her own personal assistant who dealt with all the tiresome but essential details), and the occasional buzz from meeting the famous and the notorious who made up Roth's list of clients.

Friction between Roth and Cecilia was mild, and usually limited to a brisk exchange at the start of each working day over the schedule. So it was this morning.

"Look," said Roth as they checked the first name in his appointment book, a movie actor now enjoying a second career in television. "I know he's not one of your favorite guys, but it wouldn't kill you to be nice to him. A smile, that's all."

Cecilia rolled her eyes and shuddered.

"I'm not asking for genial. I'm just asking for pleasant. What's the matter with him, anyway?"

"He calls me 'babe' and he's always trying to grab my ass."

Roth didn't blame him. In fact, he'd frequently had thoughts in that direction himself. "Boyish enthusiasm," he said. "Youthful high spirits."

"Danny." Another roll of the eyes. "He *admits* to sixty-two."

"OK, OK. I'll settle for glacial politeness. Now listen — there's a personal project you could help me with, a kind of celebrity lifestyle thing. I think it's the right moment for me."

Cecilia's eyebrows, two perfectly plucked arcs, were raised. "Who's the celebrity?"

Roth continued as though he hadn't heard her. "You know I have this fabulous wine collection?" He looked in vain for some change in Cecilia's expression, some quiver of appreciation from those impassive eyebrows. "Well, I do, and I'm prepared to give an exclusive interview, in my cellar, to the right journalist. Here's the angle: I'm not just a business machine. I'm also a connoisseur, a guy with taste who appreciates the finer things in life — châteaus, vintages, Bordeaux, all that great cobwebby French

14

shit. What do you think?"

Cecilia shrugged. "You and a hundred others. L.A. is full of wine freaks."

Roth shook his head. "You don't understand. This is a unique collection. These are first-growth Bordeaux reds from the exceptional vintages — more than five hundred bottles." He paused for emphasis. "Worth more than three million dollars."

Three million dollars was a concept Cecilia could grasp. "Cool," she said. "Now I get it."

"I'm thinking of an *L.A. Times* exclusive. Do you know anyone at the *L.A. Times*?"

Cecilia studied her nails in thought for a moment. "The owners. Well, Daddy knows the owners. I guess he could ask them about someone to put on the story."

Roth smiled, leaned back in his chair, and admired his buttercup-yellow ankles. "Terrific," he said. "Then we're all set."

The interview had been fixed for a Saturday morning, and the Roth household was briefed and ready. Michelle was to have a walk-on part at the beginning of the proceedings, playing the role of gracious hostess and, if you believed her, occasional wine widow. Rafael had been instructed to clip and reclip the purple bougainvillea that tumbled along the terrace wall. The Mercedes, glossy from its latest waxing, had been left, as if by chance, out in the driveway. In the cellar, a Mozart piano concerto drifted from speakers concealed in shadowy nooks. Evidence of wealth, taste, and refinement was everywhere. Roth had even considered opening one of his precious bottles, but in the end couldn't bring himself to make the sacrifice. The journalist and the photographer would have to make do with the Krug that was cooling in a crystal ice bucket on the cellar table.

The arrival of the *L.A. Times* was signaled by a call from the security guard at the gate. Michelle and Roth took up their positions at the top of the staircase that led down to the driveway, where they waited for the journalists to get out of their car before making their stately progress down the steps.

"Mr. Roth? Mrs. Roth? Good to meet you." A burly man in a rumpled linen jacket walked toward them, hand stretched out. "I'm Philip Evans, and this walking camera store" — he nodded toward a young man festooned with equipment — "is Dave Griffin. He does the pictures. I do the words." Evans turned on his heel until he faced south. "Wow. This is some view you have here."

Roth dismissed the view with a proprietorial wave of the hand. "Wait till you see the cellar."

Michelle glanced at her watch. "Danny, I have all those calls to make. I'll leave you boys here if you promise to save me a glass of champagne." And with a smile and a farewell flutter of her hand, she made her way back into the house.

Roth let them into the cellar, and while the photographer was wrestling with the problems of light and reflection, the interview began.

Evans was something of an old-fashioned reporter, in that he dealt with fact rather than speculation, and nearly an hour was spent covering Roth's history: early days in the entertainment business, his first encounter with fine wines, his developing passion for the great vintages, his installation of the technically perfect cellar. In the background, punctuating the sound of Mozart, were the clicks and whirrs of a camera as the photographer made his rounds.

Roth, whose business life was spent speaking on behalf of clients, found that he was relishing the novelty of talking about himself to an attentive listener. So much so that it took a question from Evans about vintage

17

champagne to remind him to open the Krug. This led, as a glass or two of champagne so often does, to a more relaxed and less discreet turn in the interview.

"So tell me, Mr. Roth," said Evans. "I know you collect these wonderful wines for pleasure, but are you ever tempted to sell? I mean, you must have a considerable amount of money tied up down here."

"Let's see," said Roth, as he looked around the racks of bottles and the neatly stacked wooden cases. "The '61 Latour, for instance, would fetch between $100,000 and $120,000 a case, the '83 Margaux around $10,000, and the '70 Pétrus — well, Pétrus is always big numbers. I guess that's worth about $30,000, if you can get it. Every time a bottle of that vintage is drunk, the scarcity pushes the price up just as much as the quality of the wine." He refilled their glasses and studied the fine spiral of bubbles rising upward. "But to answer your question: no, I'm not tempted to sell." He smiled. "To me, it's like an art collection. Liquid art."

"Ballpark figure," said Evans. "What do you think your collection is worth?"

"Right now? The Bordeaux is worth around three million. That will go up as time goes by. Like I said, scarcity pushes price."

The photographer, who had exhausted the creative possibilities of wine bottles and cellar racks, now advanced toward Roth, light meter in hand, to take a reading. "Portrait time, Mr. Roth," he said. "Could we have you over by the door, maybe holding a bottle?"

Roth thought for a moment. And then, with infinite care, took a magnum of the 1970 Pétrus from its resting place. "How about this? Ten thousand bucks, if you can ever find it."

"Perfect. Now, over to your left, so we get the light on your face, and try holding the bottle up against your shoulder." *Click click.* "Great. Bottle a bit higher. A little smile. Fabulous. Terrific." *Click click click.* And so it went on for another five minutes, giving Roth a chance to vary his expressions from happy connoisseur to serious wine investor.

Roth and Evans left the photographer to pack up his equipment and waited for him outside the cellar. "Got everything you want?" asked Roth.

"Absolutely," said the journalist. "It's going to be a really nice piece."

And so it was. A full page in the Weekend section (headlined, predictably, "The Grapes of Roth"), with a large photograph of Roth cradling his magnum and several smaller shots of the cellar, accompanied by a suitably detailed and flattering text. Not only was it flattering, but it was also filled with the kind of detail wine lovers expect, from the number of bottles produced for each vintage to tasting notes from experts like Broadbent and Parker; from grape varieties to more arcane matters like the dates when picking commenced, periods of maceration, soil conditions, and tannin content. And, sprinkled throughout the text like truffles in *foie gras,* there were the prices. These were usually expressed by the case or by the bottle, but sometimes by smaller, more affordable measures, as in $250 a glass or even (for the Yquem) $75 a sip.

Roth, after reading and rereading the article, was more than satisfied. He thought that he came across as an informed and serious man. Nothing flashy or nouveau riche, as long as the reader disregarded the passing references to the lodge in Aspen and Roth's fondness for private jets. But even these were perfectly acceptable, indeed quite normal, in the upper reaches of twenty-first-century California society. So, all in all, Roth was confident that the piece had achieved its purpose. The world — or at least the world that counted, *his* world —

had been made aware of the fact that he was not only a wealthy and successful businessman, but also an aficionado of vintages, a veritable patron of the grape.

This was confirmed many times in the days following the appearance of the article. The maître d's and sommeliers of Roth's favorite restaurants treated him with an extra touch of deference, and nodded approvingly at his choices from the wine list. Business acquaintances called him seeking advice about their own, less distinguished, cellars. Magazines requested interviews. The piece had also run in the *International Herald Tribune*, with a worldwide circulation. Over night, it seemed, Danny Roth had become the wine guy.

TWO

It was Christmas Eve in Los Angeles, and all the traditional sights of that most joyous of seasons were on display. Santas in sunglasses — some wearing red shorts as a concession to the heat — rang their bells and wagged their false beards as they set up camp in the prosperous parts of town. In Beverly Hills, a few of the more festive lawns had been dusted with artificial snow imported from China. Rodeo Drive was a-twinkle with the glint of platinum American Express cards. A bar on Wilshire was offering an extended happy hour, from eleven a.m. to midnight, with the added inducement of organic martinis. And members of the L.A. Police Department, brimming with goodwill to all men, were dispensing parking tickets and D.U.I. citations with unusual generosity.

As the dusk of evening deepened into night, an ambulance made its way through the holiday traffic on Sunset and headed into the hills before stopping at the security barrier that marked the entrance to Hollywood Heights. The guard, yawning with boredom after an uneventful few hours, emerged from his air-conditioned sentry box and peered at the two men inside the ambulance.

"What's up?"

The ambulance driver, spruce in his hospital whites, leaned out of his window. "Sounds serious, but we can't be sure until we get there. Call from the Roth residence."

The guard nodded, and went back into his miniature fortress to call the house. The driver saw him nod again before he put the phone down and the barrier went up. Recording the visit in his log, the guard checked his watch and saw that there were only ten minutes left until the end of his shift. Tough luck on his replacement, who would be spending the rest of Christmas Eve in the gatehouse, watching reruns on TV.

Arriving at Château Roth, the ambulance was met in the driveway by the man who had given the green light to the security guard, a visibly agitated Rafael. He had been left in charge of the property while the owners spent Christmas in Aspen, and only the thought of vanishing across the Mexican border with $50,000 in cash had persuaded him to abandon his comfortable, if undeclared, employment. He took the two ambulance men down to the cellar and let them in.

Unhurried and methodical, they pulled on rubber gloves before unloading empty cardboard cartons bearing the name of a winery in the Napa Valley. A preliminary tour of the cellar showed that the bottles of Bordeaux occupied a separate section, which was helpful. They would need to spend less time looking through the storage racks. Working from their list, they began to pack bottles into the cartons, ticking off names and vintages as they packed. Rafael was kept busy putting the filled cartons into the back of the ambulance, with a warning that any breakages would cost him dearly.

Each carton held either a dozen bottles or six magnums, and by the time the men had finished, forty-five cartons had been filled and loaded. After one last check, and a regretful glance at Roth's California wines and his boxes of pre-Castro Havanas, they switched off the cellar lights and closed the door. Now it was time to make a few adjustments to the interior décor of the ambulance.

The cartons were stacked neatly on either side of a stretcher bed before being covered with hospital blankets. Rafael, by now so nervous that he was very close to being a genuine emergency case himself, was tucked into the stretcher bed and hooked up to a fake morphine drip that would alleviate the pain of his fake burst appendix. Thus prepared, the ambulance drove down to the security gatehouse, pausing only long enough to wish the guard a brisk Merry Christmas before disappearing, lights flashing, into the night.

The driver grinned as he heard sounds of movement from the back of the ambulance. "OK, Rafael, time to get up. We're going to drop you off before we get on the freeway." He took an envelope from his pocket and passed it back over his shoulder. "Better count this. It's all in hundreds."

Five minutes later, the ambulance pulled into a dark side street to let Rafael out. Next stop was a lock-up garage on an even darker street in a run-down section of west L.A., where the cartons of wine were transferred from the ambulance to an unmarked van. All that remained was to remove the license plates from the ambulance and abandon it in a nearby hospital parking lot before the two men headed off in the van toward Santa Barbara.

THREE

Aspen had been more than usually enjoyable for Roth. Plenty of A-list names were there, skiing and being seen, and he was able to cultivate the acquaintance of three or four potential clients. This, to his surprise, was helped considerably by the *L.A. Times* piece. Even though it had appeared back in September, those A-listers who were, as they said, "into wine" were thick on the ground that year, and they had all read about Roth's collection. The traditional topics of Aspen conversation — adultery, stock tips, cosmetic surgery, studio larceny — had been replaced by talk of cellars and vintages, Bordeaux versus California, optimum aging times, and, of course, wine prices.

Roth found himself holding forth to small but rapt audiences, household names who would normally have been a little out of his social reach, and the business possibilities were not lost on him. It might be wine today, but it could easily be a juicy contractual crisis tomorrow. Throughout that snowy Christmas week Roth's skis lay untouched, and Michelle had their personal ski instructor all to herself.

The Roths shared a jet on the way home with a couple whom they knew slightly from L.A., and who had been wildly impressed to see Roth in such celebrated company. Roth waved away their flattery and complained, in a good-natured way, of being kept far too busy to ski. The implication was that he had been talking business, not Bordeaux, and Roth was happy to leave it like that. It was a satisfactory end to a most satisfactory week.

His good mood lasted until the evening, when he and his wife arrived back at the house in Hollywood Heights and found that Rafael wasn't there to greet them. Nor had he left a note to explain his absence. It was unusual, and worrying. But as they went from room to room they began to relax. The Warhols were on the walls, the Giacometti was stalking across the terrace, and the house seemed to have been untouched. In Rafael's tiny basement apartment, his clothes were still hanging in the closet and his bed was neatly made. There was no sign of a sudden departure. The Roths went to bed early, puzzled, irritated, but not unduly worried.

It wasn't until the following morning that Roth went down to the cellar.

"Jesus *Christ!*" The bellow of anguish almost caused Michelle to fall off her Stair-Master. She hurried down to the cellar, where she found Roth staring, as if hypnotized, at a wall of completely empty wine racks.

"My Bordeaux! Every goddamn bottle! All gone." Roth began to pace back and forth, fists clenching and unclenching in fury. A hirsute man would have been tearing his hair out. "If I catch that little son of a bitch, I'll kill him. I'll tear his heart out." Muttering ever more grisly death threats, he went upstairs in search of his BlackBerry.

In quick succession, he called the security guard at the gatehouse, the L.A.P.D., and his insurance company.

The guard was the first to arrive, clutching his logbook. By now, Roth had more or less regained the power of coherent speech. "OK. I want to know who got into my house and when, and why the fuck they weren't stopped at the gate." His finger jabbed the guard's chest. "And I want to know the name of the asshole who was supposed to be on duty."

"I'm on it, Mr. Roth." The guard, with a silent prayer that he hadn't been on duty at the time, consulted his log, finally looking up, triumph mixed with relief. "I got it. Christmas Eve, some kind of medical emergency. An ambulance came through at 8:20, left at 10:50. Tom was on duty. Your caretaker gave him the OK."

"I'll bet he did, the little shit." Roth took the logbook from the guard and peered at it as if hoping for further revelations. "That's it? No hospital name? No medical I.D.? Jesus."

"We got the license number. And I guess they said it was an emergency."

"Yeah, right. Couldn't wait to get their hands on my wine." Roth shook his head and handed the logbook back to the guard, who made a deferential exit. He got back to the gatehouse just as the police arrived: two bored-looking detectives out on an errand that they already sensed would be a waste of their time.

"OK," said Roth when they arrived at the house. "I'm a generous contributor to the P.B.A., so it would be nice for once to get something for my money. Follow me." The detectives nodded in unison, the same thought going through their minds. Here

30

was another big shot who sent the Police Benevolent Association a check each Christmas for $100 and expected special treatment.

They were hardly through the cellar door before Roth started. "See that?" he said, pointing at the empty racks. "Three million bucks' worth of wine, took me ten years to collect, impossible to replace. Impossible. And those bastards knew what they were doing. They only took the Bordeaux."

"Mr. Roth." The older of the detectives had his notebook out while his partner started to look around the cellar. "Let me get some details. Now, when —"

"You want details? Christmas Eve, we were away, and this ambulance comes to the gate with some dumb story about an emergency. The security guy calls the house and the caretaker gives him the OK."

"Caretaker's name?"

"Torres. Rafael Torres."

"Mexican?"

"Does he sound Jewish?"

The detective sighed. A smart-ass. "Mr. Roth, I have to ask you. Did your caretaker have a green card? Social Security? In other words, was he legal?"

Roth hesitated. "Well, not exactly. But what difference does that make? He let

31

them in, and they must have taken him with them. Because when we got back from Aspen last night, he wasn't here. We checked the house. There was nothing missing. And then I looked in the cellar this morning." Roth turned to the empty racks and spread his hands. "Three million bucks."

The detective looked up from his notes, shaking his head. "Trouble is, Mr. Roth, we're now December 31. That's six clear days since the robbery. They knew what they wanted, and they worked out how to get in and take it. We'll check for prints, but . . ." He shook his head again. "This is a professional job. They won't have left their address."

It was Roth's turn to sigh. A smart-ass cop. That's all he needed.

The detective finished writing and put his notebook away. "We'll get the forensics people round here later today, and We'll check things out with the security guard. He may have noticed something about the ambulance that could give us a lead. We'll get back to you as soon as we have something. Meanwhile, I suggest you don't touch anything in the cellar."

Roth spent the rest of the morning on the phone. His first call, to Cecilia Volpé, was fielded by the receptionist. She reminded

him that he had given Cecilia compassion-
ate leave to go for hair extensions and a total
body tanning spray in preparation for her
New Year's Eve festivities. And so he was
obliged to reschedule the day's appoint-
ments himself. Michelle was spending the
day in and out of her closets, choosing a
suitable outfit for the party they were going
to that night in Beverly Hills. Roth was left
to stomp around the house, the phone stuck
to his ear. Every time he thought about his
cellar, the gaping void seemed to get bigger.
Even the view from the terrace was
shrouded in a thick coating of smog. By
early afternoon, when he was due to meet
the insurance company's representative, he
was convinced that fate had it in for him.
Self-pity was mixed with anger, and anger
was winning.

Elena Morales, the vice president in
charge of private, or noncorporate, claims
at Knox Worldwide, arrived punctually at
three p.m. Under normal circumstances,
Roth would have made an effort to charm;
Elena was — as her many admirers told her
— far too good-looking for the insurance
business. She had eyes the color of dark
chocolate, jet-black hair, and a body that
was well up to Hollywood's high standards.
Today, however, all this was wasted on Roth.

Elena just had time to give Roth her business card before he set the tone of the meeting. "I hope you're not going to give me all that usual insurance crap."

Elena was used to such reactions, and the occasional tantrums, of her wealthy clients. The rich, insulated by money and protected by privilege, were not temperamentally equipped to deal with the harsher realities of life. When faced with loss of any kind, they tended to behave like spoiled children — selfish, unreasonable, often hysterical. She'd seen it all before.

"What kind of usual insurance crap would that be, Mr. Roth?"

"You know what I mean. All that fine-print bullshit about extenuating circumstances, terms and conditions, limited liability, gaps in the coverage, acts of God, loopholes in the policy, escape clauses . . ." Roth paused for breath while he searched for more examples of the iniquitous habits of insurance companies.

Elena remained silent. Experience had taught her to let nature take its course. Clients all ran out of breath and invective sooner or later.

"Well?" said Roth. "We're not talking about peanuts here. We're talking about three million dollars."

Elena glanced at the copy she had brought with her of Roth's insurance policy. The Bordeaux, according to Roth's instructions, had been insured separately, but not quite for three million. Elena sighed. "Actually, Mr. Roth, it's down here in the contract as 2.3 million dollars. But we can discuss that later. Now, I've already been in touch with the L.A.P.D., so I know most of the details, although obviously We'll have to conduct our own full investigation."

"How many years is that going to take? The wine's gone. It was insured. What else do you need?"

Elena looked at the vein pulsing on Roth's temple, a throbbing, furious worm. "I'm afraid it's a necessary part of our claims procedure, Mr. Roth. We can't pay out substantial checks until we're satisfied with the circumstances surrounding the robbery. I'm sorry, but that's standard practice. This case is a little more complicated because the robbery was clearly made possible by a member of your household. We just need to do our due diligence, that's all."

"This is outrageous." Roth got up, walked over to where Elena was sitting, and glowered down at her. "Are you insinuating that I had something to do with this? Are you?"

Elena stood up and slipped the Roth

35

policy into her briefcase. "I'm not insinuating anything, Mr. Roth." She snapped the case shut. "I don't think we're going to get much accomplished today. Perhaps when you're less upset you'll have a chance to consider —"

"I'll tell you what I've had a chance to consider. I've had three million dollars' worth of wine stolen, and you and your goddamn procedures and cockamamie standard practices are doing your level best to duck your legal responsibilities. I want my wine back, or I want a certified check for three million dollars. Is that clear?"

Elena made for the door. "Quite clear, Mr. Roth. Our investigator will be getting in touch with you. Happy New Year."

I shouldn't have said that, Elena thought, as she was driving back to her office. Right now, he's probably having a heart attack. Not for the first time, she wondered whether the money she was paid made up for the arrogance and dishonesty she had to tolerate. The nerve of the guy, trying to bump up the insured value of his wine by seven hundred grand. Her cell phone rang. It was her boss.

"Roth's been on the phone. It sounds like it wasn't a great meeting. Let's talk when you get back to the office."

The president of Knox Worldwide, an elderly man whose benign appearance concealed a keen mind and a professional reluctance to pay out money, stood up when Elena came into his office. It was one of the things she liked about Frank Knox, a touch of courtesy in an increasingly ill-mannered world. He came around his desk and they settled into two battered leather club chairs next to the window. It was a minor source of pride to Knox that he hadn't changed the décor of his office for thirty-five years. The massive partner's desk, the heavy walnut bookcases, the fine old oriental rugs (now wearing a little thin on top), and the cracked oil paintings of stags and other noble creatures — they were all part of a previous century. Like Knox himself, they were elegant, well-worn, and comfortable.

He grinned at her. "Another fun-filled day in Hollywood. Tell me about it."

Elena went over what she had learned from the detective handling the case, and gave Frank a brief account of Roth's behavior, including his attempt to inflate the insured value of his wine. "Frank, believe me. He was practically foaming at the mouth. He wasn't making sense. There was no point in my staying."

The old man nodded. "I got some of that

when he called me." He gazed out of the window, his fingers tapping the arm of his chair. "Now let's see. The robbery took place six days ago, plenty of time for everyone to get away. The police reckon they were pros. It was an inside job, made possible by an illegal immigrant. I'd say there's no chance of tracing him. And there's our friend Mr. Roth, jumping up and down for a certified check."

"For three million," Elena said.

"He wishes. Unfortunately for him, he only paid the premium for 2.3 million. Even so, an amount like that has considerable sentimental value, and I'd hate to part with it." The old man leaned forward. "How many bottles did you say were stolen?"

"Between five and six hundred — that's if you believe Roth."

"Well, that's going to take some time to drink. Maybe that's what we should be looking for: not the crooks, but the wine. Getting rid of five hundred bottles won't be easy, unless they did the job on commission." He stood up, and smiled at Elena. "We need a bloodhound. Got any ideas?"

FOUR

Elena sat at her desk and considered the options. If her recent conversation with the police was anything to go by, the L.A.P.D. was unlikely to pursue the investigation with any great zeal. The trail was already cold and there were no immediate clues. She could see the case gathering dust for years.

To help with other cases in the past, she had called in freelance claims agents, investigators who specialized in different aspects of crime and catastrophe, everything from jewelry theft to collapsing apartment buildings. But wine? She'd never had to deal with stolen wine before — and so much of it. Five hundred bottles spirited away with the efficiency of a military operation. One thing was sure: those stolen bottles weren't going to turn up on eBay. It had to be a robbery-to-order, a commission job planned and funded by God knows whom, probably another collector. If that was so, all she had to do was find a wine connoisseur with criminal tendencies. Simple. There couldn't be more than a few thousand of them scattered around the world.

A bloodhound was what Frank had said they needed. But it had to be a bloodhound with a difference; a bloodhound with imagination and unconventional contacts, ideally with firsthand experience of crooks at work.

While Elena thought, she had been flipping through her Rolodex. She stopped at the letter L. She looked at the name on the card and sighed. No doubt about it, he'd be the man for the job. But did she really want to get involved with him again? This time, keep it at arm's length and keep it businesslike, she said to herself as she buzzed her secretary.

"See if you can get me Sam Levitt, would you? He's at the Chateau Marmont."

Sam Levitt's C.V., if he had ever been foolish enough to produce one, would have made unusual reading.

As a law student at college, wondering how he was going to pay back his student loan, he developed an interest in the use of crime as a means of obtaining large amounts of money. But, not being a violent man, he was not attracted to the idea of violent crime. Too crude, too heavy-handed, and, not least of all, too damned dangerous. What appealed to him was the use of intelligence as a criminal weapon. The brain, and not the gun.

Naturally enough for a young man with nonviolent crime as a career choice, he entered the world of corporate law. He worked brutally long hours and he made money. And, thanks to the obligatory duty of entertaining clients, he acquired a taste for good food and fine wine. But there was a problem, which became worse every year. It was tedium, provoked by those very same clients: dull men who, by dint of greed and ability, had made fortunes and were determined to make more. Asset-strippers, leveraged-buyout merchants, takeover tycoons — all worshipping at the shrine of the share price. Levitt found them increasingly boring, and found his distaste for their world increasingly hard to conceal.

The final straw came during a corporate retreat weekend, an orgy of executive bonding that left him hungover and severely depressed. On impulse, he resigned and started to look around for crime of a more straightforward and, in a way, more honest sort. "Anything considered" was his new motto, providing it didn't involve guns,

41

bombs, or drugs.

This is where the imaginary Levitt C.V. becomes short on detail and a little murky. He spent some time in Russia, and came to know parts of South America and Africa quite well. He later referred to this as his import/export period, a hectic few years of great risk and great reward. It ended with a short but memorably unpleasant stay in a Congolese jail, which cost him three cracked ribs, a broken nose, and a substantial bribe to get out. The experience prompted him to think that perhaps the moment had come to make another career adjustment. Like many Americans before him seeking time and space to ponder life's important decisions, he went to Paris.

The first few weeks were spent catching up on girls and gastronomy after the deprivations of Africa. It wasn't long before Paris made him realize how little he knew about something he enjoyed so much: wine. Like most amateurs with a receptive palate, he could tell good from ordinary, and exceptional from good. But often there were times when the seductive whisperings of sommeliers were beyond him. Parisian wine lists, too, were filled with unfamiliar châteaus. It was frustrating. He wanted to know, not guess. And so, having both time and money on his hands, he decided to treat himself to a six-month course at the Université du Vin at Suze-la-Rousse, an establishment of higher learning conveniently situated in Côtes-du-Rhône country.

He found that it was a distinct improvement on law school. The subject itself, of course, was much more agreeable. His cosmopolitan fellow students — French, English, Chinese, some Indian pioneers, and the inevitable Scot — were much more interesting. The field trips to Hermitage (home of the "manliest" wines on earth), Côte-Rôtie, Cornas, and Châteauneuf-du-Pape were delicious and instructive. He began to pick up some French, and he even briefly thought of buying a vineyard. The time passed quickly.

But he wasn't ready to bury himself in the French countryside, and after years of traveling he was feeling the tug of America. How had it changed while he'd been away? How had he changed?

In one respect, not at all. His fascination for the ingenious, bloodless crime remained, and as the end of his course drew near his thoughts turned more and more frequently to the idea of going back to work — but with a difference. Memories of the Congolese jail were still vivid. This time, he thought, he would operate on the legitimate side of the fence, as an investigator and a consultant on criminal matters. Or, as he liked to think of it, a poacher turned gamekeeper.

For a man who liked the sunshine life, the choice of Los Angeles as a base was almost inevitable. L.A. had everything: delightful climate, money and extravagance, a high incidence of multimillionaires involved in dubious deals, the wretched excesses of the movie business, an abundance of pretty girls and celebrities — all the ingredients for mischief and amusement were there. And it took only a short reconnaissance before he found the ideal place to live.

The Chateau Marmont, tucked away off Sunset Boulevard in West Hollywood, was intended to be L.A.'s first earthquake-proof apartment building. Alas, it opened in 1929, when the financial tremors from Wall Street and the Depression made selling apartments impossible. Rooms were an easier sale, and so the Chateau became a hotel with apartment-sized suites.

This, for Sam, was one of its great attractions, but there were many more: the absence of domestic responsibilities, the charm and efficiency of the staff, the discreet entrance, the convenient location, the relaxed atmosphere. Unlike most modern formula hotels, the Chateau had character, a distinct personality. And there were suites available for permanent guests, the lifers. After a trial stay, Sam became one of them. He moved into a suite on the sixth floor and started looking for clients, which wasn't too difficult in L.A. Somebody rich was always in trouble.

The fact that money wasn't a problem allowed him to choose only those cases that interested him: the more unusual swindles and scams, the more mysterious disappearances and hoaxes, the more daring high-end robberies. He had found his niche, and it wasn't long before he had gained a reputation in certain circles as a man who got results and kept his mouth shut.

Elena's call came through as he was recovering from a vigorous half hour in the hotel's attic gym.

"Sam, it's Elena." She hesitated. "Sam, am I interrupting something? You're out of breath."

"It's the sound of your voice, Elena. Always does it to me. How are you?"

"Busy. That's why I'm calling. I need to talk to you. Can you do lunch tomorrow?"

"Sure. Do you want to come up to the

apartment? Just like old times?"

"No, Sam. I'm not coming up to the apartment, and it's not going to be just like old times. It's work. Remember, work."

"You're a hard-hearted woman. I'll make a reservation downstairs for 12:30. Hey, Elena?"

"What?"

"It will be good to see you again. It's been a long time."

They were both smiling as they put down their phones.

Sam had reserved his usual table, which was set apart and partially screened from general view by the exuberant plant growth that made the courtyard such a green and pleasant place. He watched as Elena was shown to the table, and saw heads turn as everybody else took a long look at her. Was she famous? Who was she meeting? You never knew at the Chateau. Celebrity sightings were part of the décor.

Sam kissed her on both cheeks and stepped back, inhaling deeply. "Mmm. Still wearing Chanel No. 19."

Elena looked at him, her head tilted to one side. "Still haven't had your nose fixed."

As they ate (Caesar salad and Evian for Elena; salmon and Meursault for Sam), Elena went through everything she knew about the robbery. Over coffee, she gave Sam photocopies of the *L.A. Times* article and the detailed list of stolen wines that Roth had supplied. Watching Sam as he skimmed through them, she had to admit that the broken nose should probably stay broken. It saved him from being handsome.

Sam looked up from the list. "These are some serious wines. Interesting that they didn't steal anything from California. Anyway, I take my hat off to whoever organized it. Well timed, well planned, nice and clean — my kind of job."

Elena looked at him over the top of her sunglasses. "Sam?"

He laughed and shook his head. "Nothing to do with me, I promise. I never even saw the article. Besides, you know me. I work for the good guys now."

"Does that mean you'll take it on?"

"Anything for you, Elena. Oh, plus expenses, and five percent of the value of anything recovered."

"Two and a half."

"Three."

After seeing Elena out, Sam went back to his table and sat over another espresso. It had been six months since he'd seen her; six months since the evening that had ended in a verbal slugging match. Now he couldn't even remember what they'd been arguing about. His reluctance to commit? Her refusal to compromise? Anyway, it had ended badly. And it was made worse when he found out that she'd taken up with one of those pretty young actors, so numerous in Hollywood, who make a career of being not quite famous.

As it happened, Elena was thinking about that same young actor as she drove back to her office. Not one of her best decisions, she had to admit. A rebound that hadn't bounced. Not quite soon enough, she had realized that her new friend was already conducting a passionate love affair with himself, and if ever the conversation showed signs of turning away from that all-consuming subject, his eyes would either glaze over or seek reassurance in the nearest mirror. How long had that lasted? Three weeks? A month? Too long.

Elena shrugged, trying to clear her head. She was saved from her thoughts by the sound of the first few bars of "La Vie en rose." It was the ringtone Sam had put on her cell phone after a trip they'd made to Paris, and she somehow hadn't found the time to change it.

"So? Any progress?"

Elena recognized the modified snarl that Danny Roth used when talking to underlings. She braced herself before replying. "I think so, Mr. Roth. We've just retained a specialist investigator who will be working exclusively on your case."

"OK. Tell him to call me."

FIVE

Sam's call found Cecilia Volpé in unusually good spirits, the result of her doting father's latest gift, a pearl-gray Porsche. Her normally brusque phone manner had softened to a purr, and she sounded almost apologetic when she told Sam that Mr. Roth was unavailable right now; he was taking a meeting. (In Hollywood, meetings are not held; like sleeping pills, they are taken, often with similar effects.) When Sam explained who he was and why he was calling, there was even a note of sympathy in Cecilia's reply.

"He's, like, *devastated.* I mean, three million dollars' worth of wine, plus he was *betrayed* by that little Mexican creep. Total, total bummer." She might have gone on in a similar vein if Roth himself hadn't emerged from his office with one of his younger clients, an actress who divided her time between filming and rehab. Cecilia put Sam on hold until Roth returned from escorting his youthful charge to the elevator.

"It's a Mr. Levitt. He's the investigator from the insurance company."

Roth went into his office to take the call. "About time. What have you found?"

"We've only just started looking, Mr. Roth. It would be helpful if you and I could get together, and I need to see the cellar. Any time that suits you."

"Right now suits me."

Sam took a deep breath. This was not going to be fun. "Right now is fine, Mr. Roth. I have your address. I'll be there in thirty minutes."

Sam was waiting at the gatehouse when Roth arrived forty-five minutes later, with no apologies and the most perfunctory of handshakes. It was mutual dislike at first sight. By the time Roth had led the way to the cellar, any pity Sam might have felt for the robbery victim had disappeared.

During the next half hour, Sam's attempts to gather information were continually thwarted by the demands of Roth's Black-Berry, leaving Sam free to inspect the cellar and the wine — the California Chardonnays, Cabernets, and Pinots — that remained after the robbery. Then he took a long look at the massive, Spanish-style

51

wooden door that separated the cellar from the rest of the house. Eventually, with nothing more left to inspect, he stopped directly in front of Roth, who had assumed a position of prayer — head bent, hands close together — as he worshipped his Black-Berry.

"I hate to interrupt you," said Sam, "but I'm just about through."

Roth interrupted his devotions, looking up with a frown of irritation from the tiny screen he was studying. "So? What do you think?"

"First, your security arrangements stink. I could pick the lock on that door with a nail file. Why didn't you have the cellar on a separate alarm system? Big mistake. Anyway, all that's a little late now. The police probably told you that the guys who did it were pros."

Sam stopped talking. Roth was once again consulting his electronic brain. Sam aimed his next remark at the top of Roth's shining skull.

"In a crime investigation, you should never dismiss the obvious conclusion until you've proved it wrong." Roth still didn't look up as Sam continued. "We know that this was an inside job. We know that Rafael Torres has disappeared, and we know that you were in Aspen when the robbery took place. Those are the facts, Mr. Roth, and a suspicious mind might jump to the obvious conclusion."

Roth finally put his BlackBerry in his pocket. "Which is?"

"You could have used Aspen as your alibi and set up the whole deal — stolen your own wine, paid off your caretaker, claimed the insurance, and had a fine old time drinking the evidence." Sam shrugged and smiled. "Ridiculous, I know. But it's my job to look at every possibility." He reached into his pocket. "Here's my card. I'll be in touch with any developments." He stopped at the door. "Oh, by the way. If I were you, I'd drink those bottles of Cabernet Sauvignon pretty soon. The '84 is beginning to show its age."

Sam almost felt sorry for Roth as he made his exit. But not quite.

Soon after his arrival in Los Angeles, Sam had been called in to investigate the so-called Impressionist ring, a group of high-society art dealers trading in superlative fakes of Monets, Cézannes, and Renoirs. It was during this, one of his first totally legitimate jobs, that Sam found himself working with the L.A.P.D., in the impressive shape of Lieutenant Bob Bookman. Here was a man who loved his food, and it showed. But being tall, he wore his weight well, helped by a self-imposed dress code that never varied. A generously cut black suit, a black knitted silk tie, and a white shirt. He called it undertaker chic.

His relationship with Sam got off to a promising start when they discovered a mutual interest in wine, and once the art case had been dealt with they fell into the habit of meeting every few weeks for dinner, taking turns in choosing the restaurant and selecting the wine. These were in no way business meetings, but inevitably a certain amount of underworld gossip was exchanged. It had turned out to be a pleasant and fruitful arrangement for both men.

Bookman answered Sam's call with his customary world-weary grunt.

"Booky," said Sam, "I need to pick your brains, but I'll make it pleasant for you. I'm taking the cork out of a bottle of Bâtard-Montrachet this evening, and I hate to drink alone. What do you say?"

"I could be interested. What year?"

"It's the '03. Six o'clock at the Chateau?"

"Don't overchill it."

A few minutes after six, Bookman arrived at

the door of Sam's suite. It had been a hard day of serious meetings at L.A.P.D. headquarters, and Bookman felt the need to let off a little steam. He rapped on the door and adopted his most official police officer's voice. "I know you're in there," he said. "Come out with your hands up and your pants down." A young woman passing along the corridor took a startled look at the large, black-clad figure and scuttled toward the elevator.

Sam opened the door and stood aside to let Bookman's bulk into the hallway. They went through to the small kitchen, one entire wall of which was taken up with the temperature-controlled cabinets where Sam kept wines for immediate drinking. The open bottle of Bâtard-Montrachet was in an ice bucket on the counter, next to two glasses. Bookman picked up the cork and sniffed it while Sam poured the wine.

Without speaking, they held their glasses up to the evening light coming through the window. Gently swirling the wine, they applied their noses to the heady, luscious bouquet before taking their first sip.

Bookman gave a sigh of pleasure. "Let's not send this one back." He took another, longer sip. "Isn't this the wine that Alexandre Dumas said should be drunk while kneeling, with the head bared?"

Sam grinned. "I've heard that people in Burgundy salute every time they go past the vineyard." He took the ice bucket into the living room, and the two men settled into oversized armchairs, the wine on a low table between them.

"Now," said Bookman, "let me guess why I'm here." He took another sip of wine and contemplated his glass, as if in deep thought.

"I've taken on the Roth case."

"So I heard. I had someone brief me on it before I came over. Getting anywhere?"

"My only discovery so far is that Mr. Roth is a pain in the ass. Also, he's dishonest — or trying to be. The wine's insured for 2.3 million, and he's claiming it's worth three. Which it probably is; but it wasn't insured for three. Apart from that, all I know is that it was a pro job. I'm going to check with the auction houses tomorrow, but my bet is that the wine wasn't stolen for resale. It was for a private cellar."

Bookman nodded. "Makes sense. You don't see bottles like that every day. They'd be too easily traced." He held out his glass for a refill. "You don't think Roth fixed it himself, for the insurance money?"

"No. You read that piece in the *L.A.*

Times?" Roth is the kind of guy who has to show off what he's got. Having his cellar stripped makes him look like a loser." Sam twirled the bottle in the icy water before filling his own glass. "So that's where I am right now. How about you? What have your boys come up with? Any Mexican caretakers?"

Bookman's laugh came out as more of a snort of derision. "Forget it. What do we have in this country — twelve million illegals? Probably more than half of them in California, and none of them on any computer. Believe me, that guy is either safely over the border or dead in a dumpster." There was a pause while Bookman made sure his second glass tasted as delightful as the first. "Do you want to hear the good news? We found the ambulance."

"And the bad news?"

"No plates, no prints. Wiped clean, totally clean. Those guys knew what they were doing. So far, it's a dead end, and meanwhile we have a couple of other things on our plate." He ticked them off one by one on his meaty fingers. "The governor's having Tony Blair to tea in his tent. Red-alert security operation. We've just had a celebrity suicide that's beginning to look more like a celebrity murder. Some moron with a rifle is using cars on the Santa Monica Freeway for target practice. This month's homicides are up, so we have the mayor on our case. And so it goes; business as usual. A few bottles of wine disappearing doesn't come anywhere near the top of the list." Bookman heaved his great shoulders in an apologetic shrug. "We'll do what we can to help, but you're pretty much on your own with this one."

As the level in the bottle went down, the conversation moved on to the more agreeable subjects of food, wine, and the Lakers, and the next hour passed enjoyably enough. But once Bookman had gone, Sam had to acknowledge that the investigation had hardly got off to a flying start. And, as his friend had said, he was on his own with this one.

Six

Despite what one reads in detective novels, very few crimes are solved by guesswork or hunch. Unspectacular though it might be, a patient, methodical gathering of information has caught and convicted many more crooks than the blinding flash of revelation. With that in mind, Sam settled down to the essential business of due diligence.

He started by checking with the well-known names: Sotheby's and Christie's, The Henry Wine Group, Sokolin, Acker Merrall & Condit, and the others. None of them had recently bought or been offered anything on the list of stolen wines.

He tried the smaller auction houses. He tried Robert Chadderdon and other specialty importers. He consulted Wine-Searcher, hoping to come across (among the twenty million searches made every year) someone who was seeking the particular wines and vintages in Roth's collection.

But whomever he called and wherever he looked, the result was the same: a blank.

As the days turned into weeks, his research was interrupted more and more frequently by calls from an irate Danny Roth, demanding progress reports. News of the robbery had leaked out to the Los Angeles wine community, and Roth's ego was bruised and suffering. Instead of deference and admiration, he was receiving sympathy — some of it actually genuine. Even more irritating were the cold calls from cellar security specialists offering their services. Schadenfreude, the revenge of the envious, was rife. It seemed to Roth that hardly a day went by without someone he knew mentioning the robbery with thinly disguised satisfaction. Bastards.

After enduring one especially venomous morning tirade from Roth, Sam decided to go for a swim to clear his head. As he was coming back through the garden from the hotel pool, his attention was caught by a most fetching pair of legs, and, having a connoisseur's eye for such things, he stopped to admire them. And when the owner of the legs turned around, Sam saw that it was Kate Simmons, lovelier than ever and now, to the dismay of many Los Angeles bachelors, happily married to a banker.

60

Smiling, she looked him up and down: wet, tousled hair and an old Ritz Hotel bathrobe dating from his days in Paris. "Well, Sam. As dapper as ever, I see. How are you?"

Looking at her, he felt like an uncle meeting up with a favorite niece. He was having avuncular moments quite often these days. He put it down to getting older. "Kate, what are you doing here? Got time for a cup of coffee? Glass of champagne? It's great to see you."

Still smiling, she brushed a thick strand of dark-brown hair away from her brow with the back of her hand, a gesture Sam remembered she always made when she was considering what to say. But before she had a chance to speak, Sam took her arm and steered her toward a table in the shade. "As a matter of fact," he said, "I was just thinking about you, wondering how you were." He pulled back a chair for her.

"Sam, you haven't changed at all. Still full of it." But she laughed and sat down anyway.

Over coffee, she told him about her work in movie P.R., which had brought her to the Chateau for a meeting with an implausibly well-preserved female star who was preparing to promote her latest film. This involved flying by private jet to premieres in New York, London, and Paris with her hairdresser, her nutritionist, her bodyguard, eight suitcases of clothes, and her husband of the moment. As Kate put it: traveling light, Hollywood style ("without even a psychiatrist in attendance"). Sam was happy to see that she seemed to regard this nonsense with a healthy lack of respect.

When it was Sam's turn to report on the state of his life, he told Kate about the Roth job, and was surprised to find that she was already familiar with some of the details. Her husband Richard, who was himself a wine collector in a small way, had been following the case.

"Most of the wine nuts in America will have seen the piece in the *L.A. Times,*" said Kate. "One of them might have set it up. Or maybe Roth did it himself. Why not? Stranger things have happened in L.A."

This seemed to be the prevailing theory. "Well, it's possible," said Sam, "although he's putting on a pretty convincing act of being the victim. But that could be all it is, just an act. At any rate, I guess I can't leave him off the suspect list." He shrugged. "Come to think of it, he *is* the suspect list."

"Have you looked anyplace else?"

"Such as where?"

"I don't know. Europe? Hong Kong? Russia? America's not the only country that has crooks who like a good bottle of wine." Kate finished her coffee and looked at her watch. "I'd better go." She leaned over and kissed Sam on the cheek. "Come over and have dinner with us soon. You've never met Richard. You'd like him."

"Too painful. I'd spend the whole evening wondering why you didn't marry me."

Despite herself, Kate had to smile. Shaking her head, she looked at him for a long moment before putting on her sunglasses. "You big dope. You never asked me."

Then she was gone, turning as she left the garden to wave good-bye.

Back in his suite, Sam thought how fortunate he was to remain on good terms with nearly all of the women in his life. Apart from one or two dramatic exceptions — the six-foot Ukrainian model in Moscow, the homicidal rancher's daughter in Buenos Aires, and, of course, Elena — there had been no recriminations in any of his relationships. Probably, he concluded, because they had the good sense never to take him too seriously.

As he sat at his desk and looked once again at the list of stolen wines, his mind went back to Kate's comment. Of course, she was right: America wasn't the only country that produced wine-loving criminals. But where to start looking?

He got up and went across the room to his library, a long run of floor-to-ceiling bookcases, stopping in front of the section where he kept his wine books. There, in various stages of wear and tear, were Penning-Rowsell's *The Wines of Bordeaux*, Lichine's *Encyclopedia of Wines and Spirits*, Forest's *Monseigneur Le Vin,* the current year's *Guide Hachette des Vins*, Broadbent's *Wine Tasting,* Johnson's *Wine,* Olney's *Yquem,* Lynch's *Adventures on the Wine Route,* Healy's *Stay Me with Flagons,* and a score of others collected over the years. Trailing his fingers along the spines of the books, he came to a battered copy of Duijker's *The Great Wine Chateaux of Bordeaux* and took it back to his desk, making a detour on the way to pour himself a pre-lunch glass of Chablis.

It was always a pleasure to open this book. In contrast to the ornamental and sometimes comical prose so often used by wine writers striving for effect, the text was simply written and thoroughly researched. Facts took precedence over literary flourishes. And, as a visual bonus, there were

64

photographs in full color of more than eighty châteaus, their *caves,* their vines, their cellar masters, and, in some cases, their tweed-suited, long-faced, elegant proprietors. For a lover of fine Bordeaux, it would be difficult to think of a more evocative volume.

With the list of stolen wines as his guide, Sam leafed through the pages: Lafite, Latour, Figeac, Pétrus, Margaux — famous names, legendary wines, handsome châteaus. He had always meant to explore the immaculate vineyards of Bordeaux, an area that he once heard described as a masterpiece of gardening on the grand scale. To his regret, he had never taken the time to make the trip. And it was this regret, as much as the demands of the investigation, that helped him come to a decision. He closed the book with a snap and called Elena Morales.

Her voice was slightly muffled when she answered, a sign that Sam knew well. "You uncivilized woman — you're eating lunch at your desk again. You'll get terrible indigestion."

"Thanks, Sam. You really know how to cheer a girl up. As it happens, I'm too busy to go out. How about you? Getting anywhere?"

"That's why I'm calling. I've done just about all the desk research I can do. I'm sending you a report with all the details, but don't hold your breath. I haven't come up with anything. So I've decided to do some fieldwork."

"Where's the field?"

"Elena, here's a basic rule of investigation: to arrive at an understanding of the crime, go back to the beginning. And in this case, the beginning is where the wine came from. The beginning is Bordeaux." There was silence from the other end of the line. "I thought I'd go via Paris. There's a guy there I need to see."

"Great idea, Sam, except for one thing: expenses."

"Elena, you have to speculate to accumulate."

"Listen, I know how you travel. Are you expecting us to pick up the tab for first-class airfares, fancy hotels, fancy restaurants . . ." Her voice tailed off with a sigh. "Where are you going to stay in Paris?"

"The Montalembert. Remember the Montalembert?"

"Spare me the nostalgia, Sam. We are *not* picking up your expenses."

"Let's be reasonable about this. If I find the wine, you reimburse me. If I don't find it, you don't owe me a cent. Do we have a deal?"

There was no answer from Elena.

"I'll take that as an enthusiastic yes," said Sam. "Oh, and there's one other thing. I'm going to need a fixer in Bordeaux, someone with local contacts who speaks English. I guess your Paris office can help with that. Sure you don't want to come with me?"

Thinking of Paris and looking at the plate of cottage cheese and salad on her desk, Elena thought there was nothing she'd like more. "Bon voyage, Sam. Send me a postcard."

It was nearly two years since Sam had been to Paris, and it was with a keen sense of anticipation that he made his arrangements. With hotel and flights booked, he fixed a meeting with an old sparring partner, Axel Schroeder; reserved a table for one at the Cigale Récamier; and made an appointment to drop by and see Joseph, the salesman who looked after him at Charvet.

An e-mail from Elena — its tone rather chilly, Sam thought — gave him some news from Knox's people in Paris. They recommended a Bordeaux-based agent who specialized in wine insurance, a Madame Costes. She was well connected locally, spoke good English, and, according to the Paris office, she was *très sérieuse.* Sam had learned enough about the French to know that anyone described as serious would be competent, trustworthy, and dull. In a brief exchange of e-mails, he sent Madame Costes his flight details, and she confirmed that she would meet him at Bordeaux's Mérignac airport.

Sam's final act before starting to pack was to call Roth's office.

"He's taking a meeting," said Cecilia Volpé. "Can I have him call you back?"

"Just tell him that I'm following a couple of leads, and I'm going to France for a few days."

"Cool," said Cecilia. "I love Paris."

"Me, too," said Sam. "Tell Mr. Roth I'll be in touch."

SEVEN

Waiting his turn to go through security at LAX on his way to Paris, Sam watched, with mounting sympathy, the plight of the man in front of him. He was short, plump, and jolly-looking. From the sound of his accent, he was German. He had made the mistake of smiling at the security agent and attempting a joke: "Today off with the shoes, tomorrow the underpants, eh?" The stone-faced security agent stared at him in silence. And then, clearly suspecting the poor German of trying to smuggle a potentially dangerous sense of humor onto the aircraft, ordered him to step aside and wait for the supervisor.

Shoeless and beltless, his arms raised in the crucifix position while the electronic wand was passed over his body, Sam reflected on the joys of modern travel. Overcrowded, often grubby airports, surly personnel, a better than average chance of delays, and, before every flight, the tedium and humiliation of the security check. No wonder the first thing most passengers wanted when they finally reached the plane was a drink.

The first-class cabin, a cocoon of peace after the bedlam of the terminal, came as a blessed relief. Sam accepted a glass of champagne, slipped off his shoes, and glanced at the menu. As usual, there were optimistic attempts to replicate dishes one might find in an earthbound restaurant, and today sauces were very much in favor. There were *noisettes* of lamb in a sweet spice sauce, pan-seared monkfish with a sage sauce, a vegetable pancake served over a basil cream sauce, smoked salmon cannelloni with a balsamic sauce. The menu writer, a prince of deception, made it all sound delicious. The reality, as Sam knew from past experience, would be dry and disappointing, the sauces wrinkled in shock from a blast of sudden heat, the vegetables tasting anonymous.

Why was it that airlines tried to conjure up *haute cuisine* with no more than the impossibly limited facilities of a cramped galley and a microwave? It never worked. He decided to stick to bread and cheese and good red wine, but even this was less than he had hoped for. The label on the bottle was impressive, the pedigree irreproachable, the vintage excellent. But somehow wine never tastes as it should when drunk at thirty thousand feet. With altitude, it seems to lose weight. The turbulence of flying affects the balance and flavor. In the words of an eminent critic, "After the hurly-burly of takeoff and landing, takeoff and landing, wine never has enough time to regain its composure." Sam tried one glass, switched to water, swallowed a sleeping pill instead of dessert, and didn't wake up until early morning, when the plane was beginning its descent over the English Channel.

It always felt good to be back in Paris. As his cab made its way down the Boulevard Raspail toward Saint-Germain, Sam was struck once again by the beautiful proportions established by Haussmann in the mid-nineteenth century — the generous width of the principal streets, the human-sized buildings, the magnificent gardens, and the unexpected pocket parks. Then there was the Seine and the graceful swoops of its bridges, the abundance of trees and heroic monuments, the long and majestic vistas. All these combined to make Paris one of the great walking cities of the world. And it was, by big-city standards, clean. No piles of garbage bags, no gutters choked with food wrappers and Styrofoam and crushed cigarette packets; a welcome absence of urban squalor.

Nearly two years had gone by since his last visit — a long and lovely weekend with Elena Morales — but Sam found the Montalembert to be its usual charming self. Tucked away off the Rue du Bac, the hotel is small, chic, and friendly. The younger, less grand ladies of the fashion world descend on it each year during the collections. Authors, their agents, and publishers haunt the bar, looking intense over their whisky as they brood about their royalties and the current state of French literature. Pretty girls flutter in and out. The antique dealers and gallery owners of the *quartier* drop by to celebrate a sale with a glass of champagne. People feel at home here.

Much of this, of course, is due to the staff, but it is helped also by the informal way the ground-floor area of the hotel has been laid out. In a relatively small space, a bar, a small restaurant, and a tiny library with its own wood-burning fireplace are separated not by walls but by different levels of light: brighter in the restaurant, dimmer in the library. Business lunches in the front, romantic assignations in the back.

Sam checked in, tantalized by the smell of coffee coming from the restaurant. After a quick shower and shave, he went down for *café crème* and a croissant, and went over his plans for the morning and afternoon. He was treating himself to a day off — a day of being a tourist — and it pleased him to think that his chosen destinations could be easily reached on foot: a visit to the Musée d'Orsay; a walk across the Pont Royal to the Louvre for a quick bite at the Café Marly; and a stroll through the Jardin des Tuileries on the way to the Place Vendôme and his appointment at Charvet.

The weather in Paris was hesitating somewhere between the end of winter and the beginning of spring, and as Sam walked up the Boulevard Saint-Germain he saw that the girls were of two minds about what to wear. Some were still swathed in scarves and coats and gloves; others, in defiance of the chilly breeze coming off the Seine, wore cropped jackets and short skirts. But no matter how they were dressed, they all seemed to have adopted a particular style of walking. Sam had come to think of this as a mark of the true Parisian girl: a brisk strut, head held high, bag slung from one shoulder, and — the crucial touch — arms folded in such a way that the bosom was not merely supported but emphasized, a kind of *soutien-gorge vivant,* or living bra. Pleasantly distracted, Sam almost forgot to turn in to the street that led down to the river and the Musée d'Orsay.

There was, as always, too much to take in. Sam had decided to confine himself to the upper level, where Impressionists rubbed shoulders with their Neo-Impressionist colleagues. Even so, even without paying his respects to the sculpture or the extraordinary Art Nouveau collection, more than two hours slipped by before he thought of looking at his watch. With a mental tip of his hat to Monet and Manet, to Degas and Renoir, he left the museum and headed across the river, toward the Louvre and lunch.

The French have a talent for restaurants of all sizes, and a special genius for huge spaces. La Coupole, for instance, which opened in 1927 as "the largest dining room in Paris," manages despite its vastness to retain a human scale. The Café Marly, although smaller, is still, by most restaurant standards, enormous. But it has been designed so that there are quiet corners and pockets of intimacy, and there is never a feeling that you are eating in a canteen as big as a ballroom. Best of all, there is the long, covered terrace with its view of the glass pyramid, and it was here that Sam settled himself at a small table.

Returning to Paris after a long absence, there is always a temptation to plunge in and taste everything. Call it greed, or the result of deprivation, but food in Paris is so varied, so seductive, and so artfully presented that it seems a shame not to have a dozen of Brittany's best oysters, some herb-flavored lamb from Sisteron, and two or three cheeses before attacking the desserts. But in a fit of moderation, remembering that dinner was still to come, Sam made do with a modest portion of Sevruga caviar and some chilled vodka while he watched the world go by.

Over coffee, he did his tourist's duty and wrote his ration of postcards for the day: one to Elena, telling her he was busy looking for clues; one to Bookman *(The weather is here. Wish you were beautiful);* and one to Alice, a housekeeper at the Chateau Marmont who had never ventured outside Los Angeles, but who traveled vicariously through Sam whenever he went away. He reminded himself to buy a miniature Eiffel Tower for her collection of souvenirs.

As a tentative Parisian sun broke through to brighten up the sky, he left the crowds of the Louvre for the orderly precision of the Tuileries, pausing to admire the long and extraordinary view through the gardens, along the Champs-Elysées, and all the way to the Arc de Triomphe. So far, the pleasures of the day had more than lived up to his expectations. By the time he reached the Place Vendôme he was in an expansive mood, induced by lunch and good humor — dangerously expansive, when shopping at Charvet.

Haberdashers to the gentry for more than 150 years, Charvet appealed to Sam's fondness for the understated extravagance of custom-made shirts. It was more than just a simple matter of comfort, style, and fit that he loved. It was also the whole ritual, itself an essential part of the process: the browsing over fabrics, the unhurried discussion of cuffs, collars, and cut, the certain knowledge that he would get *exactly* what he wanted. And, as a bonus, there were the stately surroundings in which these deliberations took place.

Charvet's premises — one could hardly describe them as a shop — occupy several floors of one of the most distinguished addresses in Paris: 28 Place Vendôme. No sooner was Sam inside than a figure hovering in a silky vantage point among the ties and scarves and handkerchiefs came forward to greet him. It was Joseph, who had initiated Sam some years ago into the arcane delights of single-needle stitching and genuine mother-of-pearl buttons. Together, they took the small elevator up to the fabric room on the second floor, and there, among thousands of bolts of poplin, Sea Island cotton, linen, flannel, batiste, and silk, Sam spent the rest of the afternoon. Each of the dozen shirts he eventually ordered would, like wine, be marked with its vintage, a tiny label sewn into the inner seam that identified the year in which it was made.

During his walk back to the hotel, Sam's thoughts turned to the man he was about to see. Axel Schroeder had for many years been one of the world's most successful thieves. Jewels, paintings, bearer bonds, antiques: he had stolen — or, as he preferred to put it, arranged a change of ownership for — them all. Not for himself, he was quick to point out, being a man of simple tastes, but for his acquisitive clients. Schroeder and Sam had met when they found themselves working on different aspects of the same job. A certain mutual respect had developed, and professional courtesy had since ensured that each kept well away from the other's projects. Schroeder held valid passports from three different countries, and Sam suspected that his fingerprints had been changed more than once by cosmetic surgery. He was a careful man.

Sam found him waiting in the bar of the Montalembert, a glass of champagne on the table in front of him. Slim, with a skier's tan, dressed in a pale-gray pin-striped suit of a slightly old-fashioned cut, his thinning silver hair perfectly barbered, and his nails gleaming from a recent manicure, he looked more like a retired captain of industry than the grand old man of larceny.

"Good to see you again, you old crook," said Sam as they shook hands.

Schroeder smiled. "My dear boy," he said, "flattery will get you nowhere. Have they come to their senses in Los Angeles and kicked you out?" He signaled to the waiter. "A glass of champagne for my friend, please. And make sure you put it on his bill."

Being the well-informed man that he was, Schroeder was aware that Sam had retired from a life of crime and was now fully on the legal side of the law. Not surprisingly, this tended to inhibit their conversation. For several minutes it was as if the two men were playing invisible poker, dealing pleasantries back and forth while Schroeder waited for Sam to show his hand.

"This isn't like you, Axel," Sam said. "We've been chatting for ten minutes and you haven't even asked me what I'm doing over here."

Schroeder sipped his champagne before replying. "You know me, Sam. I never like to pry. Curiosity can be very unhealthy." He took a silk handkerchief from his breast pocket and dabbed his lips. "But since you mention it — what *does* bring you to Paris? Shopping? A girl? A decent meal after all those cheeseburgers?"

Sam gave Schroeder an account of the robbery, watching him closely for any change of expression, but there was nothing. The old man stayed silent, nodding from time to time, his face inscrutable. When Sam tried to establish exactly what, if anything, Schroeder knew, even his most oblique questions were met with smiling nonanswers. A frustrating half hour passed before Sam was ready to call it a day. As they got up to leave, he tried one last long shot.

"Axel, we go back a long way. You can trust me to keep you out of it. Who hired you?"

Schroeder's face was a study in baffled innocence. He frowned and shook his head. "My dear boy, I don't know what you're talking about."

"You always say that."

"Yes, I always say that." He grinned, and clapped Sam on the shoulder. "But for old times' sake, I'll make a few inquiries. I'll let you know if anything turns up."

Sam watched through the window as Schroeder ducked into the back of a waiting Mercedes. As the car pulled away, Sam could see that he had his cell phone to his ear. Was the old rogue pretending to know nothing? Or was he pretending to know a lot more than he was prepared to reveal? There would be plenty of time to think about that over dinner.

As the final indulgence of his day off, Sam was going to the Cigale Récamier for an early dinner, and he was going to dine alone. This was for him another small pleasure, summed up by a phrase he had first encountered while he was taking the wine course at Suze-la-Rousse. It had originated with the financier Nubar Gulbenkian, whose firm belief was that the ideal number for dinner is two: "Myself and the sommelier." (The sommelier was Sam's personal variation. Gulbenkian had specified a headwaiter.)

In today's gregarious world, the solitary diner is a misunderstood figure. He might even be the object of some pity, since popular opinion finds it hard to accept that anyone would choose to sit alone in a crowded restaurant. And yet, for those who are comfortable in their own company, there is a lot to be said for a table for one. Without the distraction of a companion, food and wine can be given the attention they deserve. Eavesdropping is often rewarded by the fascinating indiscretions that drift across from neighboring tables. And, of course, a keen observer can enjoy the sideshow provided by the other diners, essential viewing for anyone amused and intrigued by the ever-changing mosaic of human behavior.

The Cigale Récamier, a five-minute stroll from the hotel, was one of Sam's favorite stops in Paris. Hidden away at the end of a cul-de-sac off the Rue de Sèvres, it had all the qualities he liked in a restaurant. It was simple, unpretentious, and highly professional. The waiters had been there forever; they knew their métier to a fault and the wine list by heart. The clientele was an interesting mixture — Sam had seen government ministers, top international tennis players, and movie actors among the Parisian regulars. And then there were the soufflés, airy and delicate, savory and sweet. If these were your particular weakness, you could make an entire meal out of them.

Sam was shown to a small table in front of the wide pillar that took up part of the center of the room. Seated with his back to the pillar, he was facing a row of tables set against a wall that was mostly mirror. Thus he could see the comings and goings behind him as well as his fellow diners across the way. A perfect spot for the restaurant voyeur.

His waiter brought a glass of Chablis and the menu, and pointed out the blackboard listing the specials of the day. Sam chose lamb chops — simple, honest, rosy, perfectly cooked lamb chops, to be followed by a little cheese and then a caramel soufflé. The choice of wine he left to the waiter, knowing that he was in good hands. With a small sigh of satisfaction, he leaned back in his chair as his thoughts turned to the last dinner he had eaten before leaving Los Angeles.

It had been one of his regular outings with Bookman. They had decided to try a wildly fashionable restaurant in Santa Monica, a temple dedicated to the extremes of fusion cuisine and daring culinary experimentation. It was, according to one breathless restaurant review, a gastronomic laboratory. They should have known better. There were multiple tiny courses — some of which arrived perched on a teaspoon, others contained in a glass eyedropper. Sauces were served in a syringe, and precise instructions were given, by a rather precious waiter, as to exactly how to eat each course. As the meal tiptoed from one edible bijou to the next, Bookman became increasingly morose. He asked for bread, only to be told that the chef didn't approve of bread with his cooking. Bookman's patience was finally exhausted when the waiter went into raptures about the *dessert du jour,* which was bacon-and-egg ice cream. That did it for both of them. They left and went off to find something to eat.

The tables around Sam were beginning to fill up, and his eye was caught by the couple sitting side by side at a table opposite him. The man was middle-aged, nicely dressed, and seemed to be well known by the waiters. His companion was an exquisite girl of perhaps eighteen, with a face like a young Jeanne Moreau. She was listening intently to what the man was saying. They sat very close to one another, sharing the same menu. Sam realized that he was staring.

"Elle est mignonne, eh?" said Sam's waiter, cocking an eyebrow toward the girl as he arrived with the lamb chops. Sam nodded,

83

and the waiter lowered his voice. "Monsieur is an old client of ours, and the girl is his daughter. He is teaching her how to have dinner with a man." Only in France, Sam thought. Only in France.

Later, as he took a turn around the side streets on the way back to the hotel, Sam reflected on his off-duty day. From Manet and Monet to the lamb chops and the memorable caramel soufflé, it had been a voyage of rediscovery mixed with frequent twinges of nostalgia. Despite the absence of leaves on the trees, Paris looked ravishing. The Parisians, who seemed to be in danger of losing their reputation for arrogance and *froideur,* had been affable. The music of the French language spoken around him, the warm whiff of freshly baked bread from the *boulangeries,* the steel-gray glint of the Seine — it was all as he remembered it. And yet, somehow, it felt new. Paris does that to you.

It had been a day well spent. Pleasantly weary, he soaked the jet lag out of his bones in a hot tub and slept like a stone.

EIGHT

The next day, during the short flight down to Bordeaux, Sam passed the time by considering the differences between a plane full of Frenchmen and a plane full of Americans. Settling into his seat, his first impression was that the sound level in the cabin was lower. Conversations were muted, reflecting the French horror of being overheard. The passengers were smaller and darker; there were fewer blonds of either sex. There were also fewer iPods, but more books. The American addiction to drinking bottled water throughout the day hadn't yet reached the French passengers (although since many of them were from Bordeaux it was possible that, for medical reasons, they restricted themselves to wine). There was no snacking. Sartorially, the style was somewhere between a day at the office and a day of bird hunting. Moss-colored, hip-length shooting jackets were worn over business suits, and

Sam half expected to see the head of a dead pheasant poking out of a side pocket. Men's hair was longer, and there were significant gusts of aftershave, but there were no masculine earrings or baseball caps to be seen. In general, the look was more formal.

There was, however, one overwhelming similarity between the Frenchman and his American cousin. Once the plane had reached the arrivals gate, two hundred cell phones appeared, as if on a preordained maneuver, so that passengers could tell wives, mistresses, lovers, secretaries, and business colleagues that, yet again, the pilot had foiled death and had managed a safe landing. Sam, who tended to agree with the theory that ninety percent of cell phone calls were unnecessary, was happy to wait for his bag in silence, a mute among babblers.

Looking for his contact, Madame Costes, he scanned the crowd in the arrivals area until his eye fell on a woman standing alone. She was holding a piece of cardboard with his name on it, at waist level. She looked almost as though she were embarrassed to be seen soliciting a stranger off a plane. He walked over to introduce himself.

Madame Costes was a pleasant surprise — not at all the sturdy old matron with flat feet and a faint moustache that Sam had anticipated. She was slim, in her midthirties, simply dressed in sweater and slacks, a silk scarf knotted loosely around her neck. Her sunglasses were pushed up into tawny, not-quite-blond hair. Her face was the kind one sees in society magazines: long and narrow and well-bred. In short, she was a prime example of *bon chic bon genre.* On his previous visits to France, Sam had often heard the phrase — usually abbreviated to *BCBG* — used to describe people of a certain class and style: they were chic, they were conservative, and they were devoted to anything made by Hermès.

Sam smiled as he took her hand. "Thanks for coming out to meet me. I hope it hasn't messed up your afternoon."

"Of course not. It's good to get out of the office. Welcome to Bordeaux, Mr. Levitt."

"Please. Sam."

She tilted her head and raised her eyebrows, as if taken by surprise at such instant familiarity. But then, he was American. "I am Sophie. Come — we find the car just outside."

She led the way out of the terminal, fishing for the car keys in the depths of a large leather bag the color and texture of a well-worn saddle. Sam was expecting her car to be the standard-issue French model: small,

87

lively, and impossibly cramped for anyone with American-length legs. Instead, they stopped at a dark-green, mud-spattered Range Rover.

Sophie clicked her tongue in disapproval. "You must forgive the car," she said. "I have been in the country yesterday. Mud everywhere."

Sam grinned. "In L.A., the highway patrol would probably pull you over for driving an unhygienic vehicle."

"*Ah bon?* Pull me over?"

"Just kidding." Sam settled back into his seat as Sophie, driving quickly and decisively, negotiated the airport traffic. Her hands on the wheel were as *BCBG* as the rest of her — polished but unvarnished nails cut short, a small gold signet ring on the little finger, so old that the family crest had worn smooth, and a vintage Cartier tank watch with a black crocodile strap.

"I made a reservation for you at the Splendide," Sophie said. "It's in the old part of town, near the Maison du Vin. I hope that's good for you. Difficult for me to know, because I live here. I never stay in Bordeaux hotels."

"Have you been here long?"

"I was born in Pauillac, about fifty kilometers from Bordeaux. So — *une fille du coin,* a local girl."

"And your English? Don't tell me that comes from Pauillac."

"Years ago, I spent some time in London. In those days, one had to speak English; nobody spoke French. Today London is almost like *une ville française.* More than three hundred thousand French people live there. They say it's easier for business." Sophie leaned forward over the wheel. "Now, no more questions. I have to concentrate."

Sophie threaded her way through a web of one-way streets and pulled up outside the hotel, an eighteenth-century building with a pompous façade and an air of self-satisfied respectability.

"Voilà," she said. "I need to go back to the office, but we can meet for dinner if you like."

Sam nodded and smiled. "I would like."

Waiting for her in the hotel lounge — or, as the official description in the hotel brochure put it, the *salon bourgeois "cosy"* — Sam felt both relieved and encouraged by his first exposure to Sophie Costes. It was entirely unworthy and chauvinistic of him, he knew, but he was much happier working with good-looking women. And he was encouraged by the fact that Sophie was a born and bred Bordelaise. From everything he had read about Bordeaux society, it was a maze of family connections and disconnections, feuds and alliances that had been developed over a couple of centuries. An insider as a guide was going to be invaluable.

The click of high heels across the floor announced Sophie's arrival. She had changed for dinner. A little black dress, *naturellement.* Two strands of pearls. A heavy black cashmere shawl. An interesting hint of scent. Sam straightened his tie.

"I'm glad I wore a suit," he said.

Sophie laughed. "What do men normally wear to go out to dinner in Los Angeles?"

"Oh, five-hundred-dollar jeans, snakeskin cowboy boots, Armani T-shirts, silk jackets, Louis Vuitton baseball caps — you know, rough country clothes. But no pearls. Real men don't do pearls."

Sophie looked as though this last piece of information confirmed a previous impression. "I think you are not a serious man."

"I try not to be," Sam admitted, "but I can get very serious about dinner. Where are we going? Should I get a cab?"

"We can walk. It's just around the corner — a little place, but the food is good and so is the wine list." Sophie turned to look up at Sam as they went down the street. "You do drink wine, don't you?"

"And how. What were you expecting me to drink? Diet Coke? Iced tea?"

Sophie waved the question away. "One never knows with Americans."

Sam liked the restaurant at first sight. It was snug, not much bigger than his living room at the Chateau Marmont, with a tiny bar at one end, mirrors and framed black-and-white portrait photographs along the walls, unfussy furniture, and thick, white tablecloths. A dark-haired, smiling woman came forward to greet them, and was introduced to Sam as Delphine, the chef's wife. Judging by the exchange of kisses between the two women it seemed that Sophie was a regular client. Delphine showed them to a corner table, suggested a glass of champagne while they studied the menu, and bustled back to the kitchen.

"This is exactly my kind of place," said Sam as he looked around. "Great choice." He nodded toward the wall opposite them. "Tell me, who are those guys in the photographs?"

"They're *vignerons,* friends of Olivier, the chef. You will see their wines on the list. Don't be disappointed if you don't find anything from California."

Delphine arrived with the champagne and the menus. Sam raised his glass. "Thanks for agreeing to help me out. It's made the job a whole lot nicer."

Sophie inclined her head. "You must tell me about it. But first, we choose."

She watched as Sam went immediately to the wine list. "You're like my grandfather. He always picked the wine first, and then the food."

"Smart guy," said Sam, with his nose deep in the list. "Well, this must be my lucky night. Look what I found — an '85 Lynch-Bages. How can we not have that? It's from your hometown." He grinned at Sophie. "Now, what would your grandfather eat to go with it?"

Sophie closed her menu. "No question. Breast of duck, cooked pink. Perhaps some oysters to start, with another glass of champagne?"

Sam looked at her as he closed the wine list, his mind going back to dinners in L.A. with girls who felt gastronomically challenged by anything more substantial than two shrimps and a lettuce leaf. What a pleasure it was to share a meal with a woman who liked her food.

Delphine took their order and came back almost immediately with the wine and a decanter. She presented the bottle to Sam for his nod of approval, removed the top of the capsule, drew out the cork — the extra-long cork, dark and moist — sniffed it, wiped the neck of the bottle, and decanted the wine.

"How do they feel about screw-top bottles in Bordeaux?" Despite the practical advantages, Sam hated the idea of wonderful wine suffering such an indignity.

Sophie allowed herself a small shudder at the thought. "I know. Some people are doing it here. But most of us are very traditional. I think it will be a long time before we put our wine in lemonade bottles."

"Glad to hear it. I guess I'm a cork snob." Sam reached into his pocket and took out a pad on which he'd made some notes. "Shall we do a little business before the oysters? I don't know how much the people in Paris told you."

Sophie listened attentively while Sam took her quickly through the robbery and the fruitless background checks that had led to his decision to come to Bordeaux. He was about to suggest a plan of action when the oysters arrived — two dozen of them, giving off a whiff of the sea, accompanied by thin slices of brown bread and the second round of champagne.

Sophie took her first oyster from its shell and held it in her mouth for a moment before swallowing. Then she picked up the shell, tilting her head back to expose the slender column of her neck, and sucked out the juice. It was a performance that Sam found extremely distracting.

Sophie realized that she was being watched. "You're staring," she said.

"I was admiring your technique. I can never do that without getting the juice on my chin."

Sophie reached for her second oyster. "Very simple," she said. "For the juice, you must make your mouth like this." She pursed her lips and pushed them forward until they made an O. "Bring the shell up until it touches your bottom lip. Make your head go back, a little suck, *et voilà.* No juice on the chin. Now you try."

Sam tried, and tried again, and by his fourth attempt Sophie judged him to be safe with oysters. The educational interlude had encouraged her to relax, and she became inquisitive, asking Sam where he had learned enough about Bordeaux to recognize a gem on the wine list when he saw it. From there, the conversation flowed, and by the time the duck arrived they were pleasantly at ease with one another.

Sam set about the ritual of tasting the wine, conscious of the expert eye watching him. He held his glass to the light to study the color. He swirled the wine gently. He sniffed; not once, not twice, but three times. He sipped, and waited for a few reflective seconds before swallowing. He looked at Sophie and tapped the rim of his glass.

"Poetry in a bottle," he said, his voice low with mock reverence. "Robust but elegant. Hints of pencil shavings — and what's this? Do I detect just a *soupçon* of tobacco? Beautifully constructed, long finish." His voice returned to normal. "How am I doing so far?"

"Pas mal," said Sophie. "Much better than you were with oysters."

They ate and drank slowly, and Sophie told Sam one of her favorite wine stories, which happened to take place in a restaurant in America. The customers had ordered a bottle of '82 Pétrus, priced at six thousand dollars. This was drunk with due respect and enjoyment. A second bottle was ordered, for another six thousand dollars. But this one tasted different, noticeably different, and it was sent back. The restaurant owner, suitably apologetic, provided a third bottle of '82 Pétrus. Happily, it was reckoned to be just as good as the first.

After the diners had left, the puzzled restaurant owner took the three bottles to have them examined by an expert, who identified the problem with the second bottle. Unlike the other two, it was genuine.

"I know why you like that story," said Sam. "Because it shows how dumb Americans can be about wine." He wagged a finger at Sophie. "I have two words for you: Robert Parker."

She was shaking her head before he had finished. "No, no, not at all. This could happen in France. You must know about the blind tasting here when the tasters mistook a room temperature white for a red. No, it's a good story because it makes a point." She picked up her glass and cupped it between both hands. "There's no such thing as a perfect palate."

Sam wasn't convinced, but he let it pass. He saw that there were a couple of glasses still left in the bottle, and he felt the need to do them justice. "Well, professor, what would you say to a little cheese?"

Sophie was smiling as she leaned forward. "I have one word for you," she said, wagging a finger at him. "Camembert."

And Camembert it was, delicate and salty, which they agreed was the only possible way to end the meal.

When they parted company after dinner, Sam found himself watching her walk away. A fine-looking woman, he thought. That night he dreamed of teaching Elena to eat oysters *à la française.*

Sophie had pleasant memories of her first meeting with Sam. He was good company, he seemed to know his wine, and his slightly battered appearance was not unattractive. And there were those wonderful American teeth. Perhaps this assignment wouldn't be so dull after all.

NINE

For Sam, the next two days were pleasant, instructive, and increasingly frustrating. Thanks to Sophie's contacts, they had access to all the châteaus, including those where visitors were not normally welcome. It was thanks to Sophie, too, that the estate managers and cellar masters went out of their way to be helpful. At château after château — from the magnificent Lafite Rothschild to the diminutive Pétrus — the two investigators had been courteously received. Their story was listened to with patient attention. Their questions were answered. They were even given the occasional glass of nectar. But Sam had to admit that the visits, while they had added to his wine education, had failed to produce any progress. It was a discouraging list: two days, six châteaus, six dead ends.

On the evening of the second day, feeling tired and flat, Sam and Sophie looked for consolation in the hotel bar. Champagne, that unfailing restorative, was ordered and served.

"Well, I guess that's it," said Sam, raising his glass. "I'm sorry to have wasted your time. Thanks for all your help. You were terrific."

Sophie shrugged. "At least you can tell them back in Los Angeles that you saw some of the great châteaus." She smiled at him. "Our little version of the Napa Valley."

Her cell phone rang. She looked at it, made a face, sighed, and put down her champagne. "My lawyer. Excuse me." She got up and walked away to take the call.

Sam had noticed this before in France, and couldn't make up his mind whether it was due to good manners or fear of eavesdroppers. But whenever possible, the French tried not to inflict their cell phone conversations on other people, preferring to find a private corner somewhere. It was a civilized habit that he wished his compatriots would adopt.

While he was waiting for the call to finish, he went back over the notes he'd taken during the château visits. At each château, they had asked who the regular clients were, the big buyers with serious *caves* to keep stocked. For the most part, the answers they had been given were unsurprising: Ducasse, Bocuse, Taillevent, the Elysée Palace, the Tour d'Argent, one or two private banks, half a dozen billionaires (whose names, of course, were not revealed). In other words, the usual suspects.

Sam sat and stared at his notes. And as he stared, another question occurred to him, a question that they hadn't thought of asking. He was still mentally kicking himself when Sophie came back from her call.

He leaned forward, looking as pleased as a dog that had just unearthed a previously forgotten bone. "You know those old French detective movies?"

Sophie looked blank.

"You know, when the detective remembers something he's overlooked?"

Still no reaction from Sophie.

"There's this moment of revelation. He smacks his forehead with the palm of his hand." Sam suited the action to the word. " *Zut!* he says. 'But of course!' " By now, he had a broad smile on his face.

"Zut?" said Sophie. "What is this *zut* and the head-slapping? Are you all right?"

"Sorry. Yes, I'm fine. But it just struck me that maybe we've been asking the wrong questions. Maybe we should be asking if anyone has *tried* to buy those particular vintages and been disappointed, because they've all been sold. Maybe there's an obsessive enthusiast out there, someone like that guy who wanted to line his cellar with vintages from 150 years of Latour, someone who's determined to fill the gaps in his collection at any price. That's a motive, isn't it?" His face was a hopeful question mark.

Sophie pursed her lips and nodded slowly. "It's possible," she said, "but in any case, we have nothing else to try." And besides, she thought, this was much more amusing than sitting behind a desk dealing with a *vigneron*'s insurance claim for frost damage. "Well, what do you want to do? We go again to the châteaus? It's better than the phone, I think."

"We go again to the châteaus. Bright and early tomorrow morning."

Sophie looked at her watch, frowned, and picked up her handbag. "I'm going to be late for my meeting, and my lawyer charges by the minute. So tomorrow — shall I come for you at ten?"

"Is that bright and early?"

"Sam. This is France."

Sam woke early. The night before, there had been second thoughts, worries about drag-

101

ging Sophie out for another day of dead ends. But sleep had restored his optimism, and the sun was shining. A good omen. He decided to go out for breakfast, found a busy café opposite the Grand Théâtre, and settled down with a *café crème* and the *Herald Tribune.*

A glance at the headlines did little to improve the morning. It was business as usual throughout the world. There were more wildfires in southern California, a futile barrage of political name-calling in Washington, the ever-thickening fog of pollution in China, unrest in the Middle East, tub-thumping from Russia, alarm and despondency in Europe, and a dose of gloom from Wall Street. Scattered throughout this litany of woe were advertisements for watches and handbags, each one more ostentatious than the last. A reminder that no matter how bad the news, it would never overcome the primordial human urge to go shopping.

Sam put aside the newspaper and looked around him. The other customers appeared curiously cheerful. Eating their *tartines* and drinking their coffee, their fresh morning faces as yet unmarked by the rigors of the day ahead, they seemed unaware that, based on this morning's news, the world might well come to an end before lunchtime.

He ordered another *crème* and jotted down the wines and vintages that he was searching for: '53 Lafite, '61 Latour, '70 Pétrus, '75 Yquem, '82 Figeac, '83 Margaux. What a list. Sam couldn't help but feel that these treasures were wasted on Danny Roth. To him, they were merely bottled status, and slightly unsatisfactory status at that, since he couldn't put them on the wall for all to see. What would he do with the insurance money, Sam wondered, if the wine was never found?

His musings were interrupted by the ringing of his cell phone. It was Sophie, calling to say it was not even ten o'clock yet, and here she was already at the hotel. Bright and early, as agreed. But where was he? Did they usually sleep this late in California?

He hurried back to the hotel to find her in the lobby. She was clearly in good spirits — smiling, holding up her arm, and tapping the watch on her wrist, pleased to have arrived before him. This morning she was dressed as if she had come on horseback — close-fitting riding pants tucked into soft leather boots, a tweed hacking jacket, a silk scarf with a subtle horseshoe motif (undoubtedly Hermès) knotted around her neck. The height of equestrian chic. Sam wondered if he should whinny as he looked her up and down with an appreciative eye. This was something you didn't see every day in L.A.

"Great outfit," he said. "Too bad you forgot the spurs. Sorry to keep you waiting. Are you feeling lucky today?"

"Of course," she said. "*Très optimiste.* Today we find something. You will see." She slipped her arm through his as they walked to the car. "Shall we start with Lafite?"

During the drive up from Bordeaux to the Médoc, Sophie explained the reason for her buoyant mood. The previous evening, after leaving Sam, she had met with her lawyer, who had told her that the three-year squabble with her ex-husband was finally settled, and she would shortly be free to remarry. Terms had been agreed upon. Her ex would keep the boat that he ran as a charter business in Saint-Barth; Sophie would keep the apartment in Bordeaux. Maybe they could even be friends. Or maybe not. He had been trouble from the start, Sophie said, always running off somewhere on a boat, and usually ending up with some unsuitable girl.

"Hmm," said Sam. "Sounds like a man after my own heart."

Sophie laughed. "You like boats?"

"I prefer girls. I don't get seasick with girls."

Sophie had chosen a road that bisected flat, immaculate countryside, with ruler-straight lines of vines running off to the horizon. There were châteaus to the left of them, châteaus to the right: Léoville Barton, Latour, Pichon-Lalande, Lynch-Bages, Pontet-Canet. Sam felt as though they were driving through a top-class wine list.

"Have you ever been to the wine country in California?" he asked.

"Napa and Sonoma? No, never. Perhaps one day. Is it anything like this?"

Sam thought of the dry, brown hills, the vast modern wineries with their gift boutiques, and the busloads of visitors. "Not exactly. But some of the wine is pretty good."

"You know why that is?" Sophie didn't give him the chance to answer. "Because you have so many French making wine over there now." She grinned at him. "I am very *chauvine*. For me, French wine is best."

"Try telling that to an Italian."

"Italians make clothes and shoes. And one good cheese. Their wine . . ." Her mouth turned down, and there was a dismissive waggle from her hand. There was clearly no room for debate. Another victory, Sam thought, for the French superiority complex.

Leaving the center of Pauillac behind them, they could now see Château Lafite, standing on a low hill well back from the road. Sophie stopped the Range Rover and turned to Sam. "It's just the one question, yes? Has anyone during the past year tried to buy the '53 and been disappointed?"

"That's it," said Sam. "Here's hoping."

As the day wore on, and the first two châteaus were crossed off the list, it seemed to Sam that they were going to repeat the frustrations of the last two days. Memories were consulted, brows were furrowed, shoulders were shrugged, but — *désolé, mais non* — there was no recollection of a hopeful but disappointed purchaser.

Their luck changed on their third stop. The estate manager, a native of Pauillac and a friend of Sophie's family, thought that he remembered a visitor from the previous fall who was very specific about the vintage he was searching for; a rather stubborn gentleman, in fact, who had been reluctant to take no for an answer. He had left his business card so that he could be contacted if any bottles of that particular vintage turned up. The estate manager scratched his head and went through his desk drawers, finally fishing out an old cigar box where he kept the cards that one day he might need. He fumbled them out onto the desk — cards of customers from England and America, wine journalists from all over the world, the odd master chef, barrel makers, sommeliers — and spread them out across the desk, an impressive display of copperplate script and fine white board.

His fingers fluttered over the cards before coming to rest. *"Voilà,"* he said as he slid one card away from the others, *"un monsieur très insistant."*

Sophie and Sam leaned forward to read the card:

Florian Vial
Caviste
Groupe Reboul Palais du Pharo 13007
Marseille

Driving to the next château — the fourth of the day — Sam asked Sophie if she knew anything about the Groupe Reboul. Had she ever heard of it? Was it a wine wholesaler?

Sophie laughed. "Everyone in France knows the Groupe Reboul. It's everywhere, involved in everything." She frowned. "Except wine. I've never heard of Reboul deal-

107

ing in wine. I'll tell you about him later, but don't get too excited. It's probably just a chance visit."

But perhaps it wasn't, because at Figeac and then at Margaux they found that Monsieur Vial had been there before them, looking for the '82 of one and the '83 of the other, leaving his card at both châteaus.

As Sam said to Sophie, "Twice could be coincidence. But not three times. I'll buy you dinner if you tell me all about Reboul."

TEN

Sam had always thought of himself as something of a gastronomic adventurer, ready to eat almost anything that was put in front of him: snails, frogs' legs, shark fin soup, chocolate-covered ants, clay-baked squirrel — he had sampled them all, and found them interesting, if not always to his taste. But his courage failed him when it came to that great panoply of guts and gizzards known as offal. The very mention of tripe induced a shudder. His was a classic case of not trying something because he was sure he wouldn't like it, and for more years than he could remember he had managed to avoid dishes that featured entrails of any kind. This was about to change.

Sophie had insisted that they return to Delphine's restaurant for dinner, and while they were walking there from the hotel she explained why. It was a Thursday. And every Thursday, Olivier the chef prepared his sublime *rognons de veau* — calves' kidneys — cooked in port and served with mashed potatoes that were so light and fluffy they almost floated off the plate and into your mouth. It was without doubt her favorite dish in the world. She was starting to go into the merits of the gravy when she noticed a lack of enthusiastic response from Sam, and a hint of dismay in his expression.

She stopped and turned toward him. "Ah," she said. "I forgot. Americans don't eat kidneys, do they?"

Sophie watched with amusement as Sam took a deep breath. "We're not great fans. I guess we have a problem with innards. I've never tried them."

"Innards?"

"You know — internal organs. Stomachs and livers and lungs and sweetbreads and giblets . . ."

". . . and kidneys." Sophie gave him a pitying look. How could a man have gone through life without tasting kidneys? She tapped his shoulder with an emphatic index finger. "I'll make you a deal. Try them. If you don't like them, you can have *steak frites* and I'll pay for dinner. Trust me."

Settled at their table, Sam was reaching for the wine list when Sophie's index finger struck again, this time wagging back and forth like an agitated metronome. "*Mais non,* Sam. How can you choose a wine to go with something you've never tasted?"

Sam surrendered the list and sat back as Sophie studied the pages, nibbling on her bottom lip in concentration. He wondered if she could cook, and if she did, what she wore. A silk scarf for whipping up omelettes? Pearls for dessert? Did Hermès make kitchen aprons? His thoughts were interrupted by Delphine, bearing glasses of champagne, and the two women held a murmured conference that ended with an exchange of nods and smiles.

"*Bon,*" said Sophie. "To start, blinis with caviar. Then the *rognons,* with an exceptional Pomerol, the 2002 Château L'Evangile. Is that good for you?"

"I never argue with a pretty woman who knows her kidneys."

They touched glasses, and Sophie began to tell Sam what she knew about the Groupe Reboul.

The British have Branson, she said. The Italians have Berlusconi. The French have Francis Reboul — Sissou to his friends and to the faithful journalists who have been documenting his business exploits during the past forty years. He had become a national institution, she said; or, according

111

to some, a national treasure, a flamboyant personality, a Marseille boy made good and loving every second of his success. He was comfortable with publicity. Indeed, his critics said that he was incapable of getting dressed each morning without issuing a press release about the color of his tie and the general state of his wardrobe. This, of course, endeared him to the media; he was a walking event, always good for a story.

And he was always doing a deal of some kind, Sophie said. The business empire he had built up over the years included construction, regional newspapers and radio stations, a soccer team, water treatment plants, transportation, electronics — he seemed to have a finger in everything.

Sophie paused as the blinis arrived.

"How about wine?" asked Sam. "Does he have a château or two?"

"I don't know. Not here, anyway." She took a mouthful of blini and her eyes closed for a moment. "Mmm, that's good. I hope you like caviar, Sam?"

"Love it. Doesn't everybody?"

"No. There are some strange people who don't eat innards of fish." She smiled sweetly and popped more blini into her mouth.

Sam held up his hands in surrender. "OK,

OK. So I like fish innards. Go on about Reboul."

Sophie searched her memory for the odds and ends of information about Reboul that she had picked up from the press and television. He lived in Marseille, in some sort of palace. His passion, frequently and publicly declared, was France and all things French (apart from Paris, which, like every good Marseillais, he distrusted). He even made the supreme sacrifice of paying French taxes, and gave a press conference each April to tell the world what a huge contribution he made every year to the national economy. He liked young ladies, and they made regular appearances at his side in the pages of celebrity magazines, always described by an indulgent press as his nieces. He kept two yachts: one for the summer, in Saint-Tropez, the other for the winter, in the Seychelles. And, of course, he had a private jet.

"And that's all I know," said Sophie. "If you want any more, you'll have to ask my hairdresser. She's mad about him. She thinks he should be president." She glanced over Sam's shoulder. "Close your eyes, Sam. Here come the kidneys."

Sam closed his eyes, but his nose told him that the kidneys had been placed in front of him. He lowered his head and inhaled the thick, gamy scent, more intense than any ordinary meat, warm and rich and infinitely appetizing. Perhaps he'd been wrong about offal. He opened his eyes. In the middle of the plate, a fragrant wisp of steam was rising from a volcano of mashed potatoes, its hollow top holding a pool of gravy. Surrounding the potatoes were four plump, deep-brown kidneys, each one about the size of a golf ball.

Sophie leaned across the table to put a small dollop of mustard on his plate. "Not too much of this, or it will fight with the wine. *Bon appétit.*" She sat back and watched him take his first mouthful.

He chewed. He swallowed. He pondered. He grinned. "You know, I've always said that at the end of a tough day, nothing hits the spot like kidneys cooked in port." He kissed the tips of his fingers. "Wonderful."

The kidneys and the excellent Pomerol worked their magic, and by the time he and Sophie had used the last of their bread to mop up the last of the gravy they were both in a mellow and optimistic mood. The connection with Reboul was interesting, possibly nothing more, but at least it was a lead that gave them something to work on.

"From what you tell me," said Sam, "he

has more money than he knows what to do with, he's a little eccentric, and he's a sucker for everything French. Do we know if he's serious about wine? I guess he must be, if he has a *caviste*. Does he have contacts in the States? Does he collect things apart from girls and yachts? I'd like to know more about him."

"In that case," said Sophie, "the one you should see is my cousin." She nodded and picked up her glass. "Yes, my cousin Philippe. He lives in Marseille, and he works for *La Provence*. That's the big newspaper of the region. He's a senior reporter. He will know about Reboul, and what he doesn't know he can find out. You would like him. He's a little crazy. They all are down there. They call it *fada*."

"He sounds great. Just what we need. When shall we go?"

"We?"

Sam leaned across the table, his voice grave, his expression serious. "You can't let me go without you. Marseille's a big town. I'd get lost. I'd have nobody to eat *bouillabaisse* with. And besides, the people at Knox are depending on you to follow every lead, every clue, even if it means going down to the south of France. As we say in the insurance business, it's a lousy job, but someone's got to do it."

Sophie was laughing even as she shook her head. "Do you always persuade women to do what you want?"

"Not as often as I'd like. But I keep trying. How about some of that Camembert Delphine keeps chained up in the cellar?"

"Yes to the Camembert."

And, by the time they had finished the wine and the coffee and the Calvados that Delphine pressed on them, it was yes to Marseille as well.

Sam had finished packing and was about to send himself off to sleep with a dose of CNN when his cell phone rang.

"Good afternoon, Mr. Levitt. How are you today?" The girl's voice sounded warm and perky and Californian. "I have Elena Morales for you."

Sam swallowed a yawn. "Elena, do you have any idea what time it is here?"

"Don't get mad at me, Sam. It's been one of those days. I've had Roth on my back. He came into the office and raised hell for an hour — lawyers, the media, his buddy the governor — if he'd stayed any longer I think he'd have dragged in the Supreme Court. In other words, he wants to know what's going on and he wants his money.

He asked for your number, but I told him you couldn't be contacted."

"Good girl."

"He'll be back. What am I going to tell him? Have you got anything?"

Sam recognized desperation when he heard it. Danny Roth in full cry, foaming at the mouth and spraying threats around, was enough to try the patience of a saint. It was time for what he hoped was a plausible lie.

"Listen," he said. "Tell Roth that I'm conducting negotiations with the authorities in Bordeaux, and I'm hopeful of a breakthrough within the next few days. But — and this is very important — these negotiations are delicate and *extremely* sensitive. The reputation of Bordeaux is at stake. Publicity of any sort, anywhere, will compromise everything. So no lawyers, no media, and no governor. OK?"

He could almost hear Elena's brain ticking over at the end of the line. "What's really happening, Sam?"

"Something's come up which might or might not be important, so we're going to Marseille tomorrow to check it out."

"We?"

Sam sighed. The second time tonight he'd been asked that question. "Madame Costes is coming with me. She has a contact down there who could be helpful."

"What's she like?"

"Madame Costes? Oh, fair, fat, and fifty. You know."

"Yeah, right. A babe."

"Good night, Elena."

"Good night, Sam."

ELEVEN

Sam had never been to Marseille, but he'd seen *The French Connection* and read one or two breathless articles by travel writers, and he thought he knew what to expect. There would be villainous characters — undoubtedly trainee Mafia executives — lurking on every street corner. The fish market on the Quai des Belges would be a conduit for substances not normally found inside fish: sea bass stuffed with heroin, or grouper with a cocaine garnish. Pickpockets and *voyous* of all kinds would be conveniently placed to relieve the unwary tourist of camera, wallet, or handbag. In every respect, it would echo Somerset Maugham's summing-up of the Côte d'Azur — "a sunny place for shady people." It sounded interesting.

Sophie, who had visited the city once, some years before, did little to change Sam's expectations. Compared with the ordered gentility of Bordeaux, Marseille as she remembered it was a scruffy, crowded labyrinth, teeming with raucous, often rather sinister-looking men and women. *"Louche"* was the word she used to describe both the city and its inhabitants — that is, as the dictionary puts it, "shifty, suspicious, dubious and equivocal." She wondered how her cousin Philippe could live, apparently happily, in such a place. But then, as she said to Sam, she had often thought there was a slightly *louche* side to him.

When they arrived at Marignane airport that afternoon, such dark thoughts were immediately dispelled by the dramatic, almost blinding clarity of the light, the thick Gauloise blue of the sky, and the amiable nature of the taxi driver who was taking them to their hotel. It soon became clear that he had missed his vocation; he should have been working for the tourist office. According to him, Marseille was the center of the universe, whereas Paris was no more than a pimple on the map. Marseille, having been established more than 2,600 years ago, was a treasure trove of history, tradition, and culture. The restaurants of Marseille were the reason God made fish. And the people of Marseille were the most generous and warmhearted souls one could wish to meet.

Sophie had been taking this in without comment, although her half smile and raised eyebrows suggested that she wasn't entirely convinced. She took advantage of a pause for breath to ask the driver what he thought of Francis Reboul.

"Ah, Sissou, the king of Marseille!" The driver's voice took on a respectful tone. "Now *there's* a man who should be running the country. A man of the people, despite his billions. Imagine, a man who plays *boules* with his chauffeur! A man who could live anywhere, and where does he choose to live? Not in Paris, not in Monte Carlo, not in Switzerland, but right here in Marseille, in the Palais du Pharo, where he can look out of his window and see the most beautiful view in the world — the Vieux Port, the Mediterranean, the Château d'If, the magnificent church of Notre-Dame de la Garde . . . *Merde!*"

The driver stamped on his brakes and reversed, weaving backward through a chorus of horn-blowing from the oncoming flow of traffic until he reached the short driveway leading to the hotel. With apologies for having overshot the destination, he dropped them off, gave Sophie his card, beamed his appreciation of Sam's tip, and wished them a memorable stay in Marseille.

On her cousin Philippe's advice, Sophie had made reservations at the Sofitel Vieux Port, a modern hotel with a view of the twelfth-century Fort Saint-Jean, one of a trio of forts that had been built to keep pirates and seagoing Parisians at bay. Up in his room, Sam slid back the window, went out onto the terrace, and took a deep breath of salt air. Not bad, he thought, as he looked down across the sweep of the city. Not bad at all. Spring had come early to Marseille, and the reflection of sun bouncing off water seemed to have polished the air and made it glitter. The masts of hundreds of small boats made a floating forest of the port. Out to sea, the Château d'If was in silhouette, flat, sharp, and clear. Sam wondered if Reboul's view could be any better than this.

He went down to meet Sophie in the lobby, and found her pacing up and down, cell phone pressed to her ear. As she finished the call, she came over, glancing at her watch.

"That was Philippe," she said. "He suggests we meet for a drink in half an hour."

"They start early in Marseille. Is he coming here?"

Sophie sighed and shook her head. "It's never simple with Philippe. He wants to show us one of his little bars where tourists never go. It's in Le Panier. He says it's a nice walk from here, *typiquement marseillais.* Are you ready for that?"

They stopped at the front desk to pick up a map and set off down the hill toward the Vieux Port. As they walked, Sophie passed on what little she knew about Le Panier. The oldest part of Marseille, once the home of fishermen, Corsicans, and Italians, it became a hiding place during the war for Jewish refugees and others trying to escape from the Nazis. In a particularly thorough act of retribution, the Nazis ordered the area to be evacuated in 1943, and then blew most of it up.

"Philippe knows many stories about that time," said Sophie. "After the war, the *quartier* was rebuilt — I would say not very beautifully — and now the people who live here are mostly Arabs."

They were crossing the quay at the end of the Vieux Port, making their way through the knots of tourists and students who were waiting for the ferry that would take them to the Château d'If. A row of old men, blinking like lizards in the sun, perched on a low wall looking at girls. A couple of dogs sniffed around the area where the fish market had been that morning. Infants in strollers took the air while their mothers chatted. It was a wholesome, peaceful scene, and Sam felt distinctly let down.

"It doesn't seem very dangerous to me," he said. "Where are all the muggers? Don't they work on Fridays? I still haven't had my pocket picked and you still have your hand-bag, and We've been in Marseille for nearly an hour. These guys are losing their touch."

Sophie patted his arm. "Don't worry. We'll ask Philippe. He can tell you where to go for a good — how do you say — mug?" She stopped to consult the map. "We need to find the Montée des Acoules, just before the cathedral. And look, this is interesting. Our closest neighbor is Reboul." She pointed to the map, and there was the Palais du Pharo, only a few hundred meters from the hotel.

The atmosphere changed as soon as they left the breezy, open spaces bordering the port. The sun disappeared. The Montée was steep and gloomy and narrow, barely the width of a car. Buildings that might have had a certain shabby charm in the sunshine looked merely drab. The only signs of life were the spicy wafts of cooking and the wail of North African pop music that came from the windows of the houses they passed. They turned left into an alley.

"I think the bar is at the end of this

street," said Sophie, "in a *placette* with no name. I don't know how Philippe finds these places."

"These *louche* guys always know the best addresses. But to be fair, you said he wanted us to see something *typiquement marseillais.*"

This caused Sophie to produce a pout with sound effects, blowing out a disdainful gust of air between pursed lips. It was a quintessentially French performance, and one that Sam had tried to emulate many times without much success. Somehow, his pouts always sounded more like flatulence than disdain. He had come to the conclusion that one needed Gallic lips.

They walked on to the end of the alley and out into a tiny square. In the middle stood a small but determined plane tree that had managed to survive despite its close-fitting collar of concrete. And in one corner, its windows covered with inspirational soccer slogans daubed in white paint — ALLEZ LES BLEUS! and DROIT AU BUT! being the favorites — was the bar. Faded letters above the entrance announced it as Le Sporting. Parked outside was a dusty black Peugeot motor scooter.

Sam pushed the door open, causing the dense haze of tobacco smoke to quiver in the current of fresh air. Conversation stopped. A group of men with ravaged, rutted faces looked up from their card game. Two others turned from the bar to stare. The only smile in the room came from a burly, dark-haired figure — a great bear of a man — sitting at a table in the corner. He stood up, spreading his arms wide, and bore down on Sophie. *"Ah, ma petite cousine,"* he said, kissing her with great enthusiasm twice on each cheek, *"enfin à Marseille. Bienvenue, bienvenue."* He turned his attention to Sam and changed languages. "And you must be American Sam." He seized Sam's hand and pumped it energetically. "Welcome to Marseille. What do you drink?" He leaned close and dropped his voice. *"Entre nous,* I would avoid the wine of the house if you want to live through the day. Pastis, perhaps? Beer? Or there is an excellent Corsican whisky. Sit down, sit down."

Sam took a look around. The décor had long ago seen better days. Most of the checkered tiles on the floor had worn through to the concrete. The ceiling, once white, was a deep, nicotine-stained brown. The tables and chairs were shiny with age. But maybe it had hidden virtues.

"Nice place," said Sam. "Do they do weddings?"

"Only funerals," said Philippe with a grin. "Apart from that, it's quiet. Very discreet. I use it for meeting local politicians who don't want to be seen talking to the press."

"Don't they have phones?"

Philippe clicked his tongue. "Phones can be tapped. You should know that, living in America." He turned around and called toward the bar. *"Mimine, s'il te plaît? On est presque mort de soif."*

"J'arrive, j'arrive." Mimine's voice, a pleasant light baritone, came from behind a wooden bead curtain at the back of the bar, immediately followed by its owner. She was an impressive sight: over six feet in her high heels, a curly mop of the kind of red hair that glows in the dark, kohl-rimmed eyes, enormous gold hoop earrings, and a truly monumental bosom, much of it visible, with the rest struggling to escape from an orange tank top two sizes too small. She stood by the table, hands on hips, her eyes fixed on Sam. Nodding toward him, she spoke to Philippe — a torrent of words delivered at breakneck speed in an accent that sounded vaguely like French, ending with a throaty cackle. Philippe laughed. Sophie blushed. Sam hadn't understood a word.

"Mimine likes the look of you," said Philippe, still laughing. "I won't tell you what she suggested, but don't worry. You're safe as long as you stay with me."

They ordered, and Mimine took much more time than necessary bending over to place Sam's pastis in front of him. For the first time in his life, he was being leered at. It was odd, but not altogether unpleasant.

"Now, Philippe," said Sophie, "stop laughing. Enough of this foolishness. Sam will tell you why we have come to Marseille."

Starting with the robbery in Los Angeles and ending with the discovery of Florian Vial's business cards in Bordeaux, Sam went through everything that he thought Philippe needed to know. The big man paid close attention, asking the occasional question and making notes from time to time. When Sam had finished, Philippe sat in silence for a few moments, tapping his pen on his notebook.

"*Bon.* Well, I can get you everything we have on Reboul, which is a lot. It's not enough, though, is it?"

Sam shook his head. "We need to see him."

"If he's here in Marseille, that's no problem. He can never resist an interview. Of course, you must have a good story."

"And we need to see his wine cellar."

"Ah. In that case, you must have a very

good story." Philippe smiled, and tapped his notebook again. "And talking of stories, there may be something in this for me." He shrugged. "You never know."

"What do you mean?"

"A scoop, my dear Sam. Isn't that the word? Let's say your investigation leads to something interesting — a little *scandale* involving the richest man in Marseille. This would be front-page news, and I would not want to share the front page with another journalist. You understand?"

"Don't worry, Philippe. We'll keep it in the family. You help us, and in return you get the exclusive." Sam extended his hand across the table. "It's a deal."

The two men shook hands, and Philippe got to his feet. "I'll go back to the office and start on Reboul's dossier. Are you going to stay here?" He winked at Sam. "I'm sure Mimine will take care of you."

"You must forgive my cousin," said Sophie, standing up and shaking her head. "Sometimes I wonder how we could be related."

Outside the bar, Philippe unlocked the padlock on his scooter and settled himself on the saddle. "The only way to get around Marseille," he said, gunning the throttle. *"A bientôt, mes enfants."* And with a wave, he clattered off down the alley, his untidy bulk balanced on two tiny wheels.

TWELVE

"So what we're looking for," said Sam, "is a cover story, something that will get us into Reboul's cellar for long enough to see exactly what he's got in there. He has a lot of wine, so that could take a couple of hours. Maybe more. We'll need to take notes, and we may need to get photographs. Oh, and it has to be a story that can't be checked quickly." He nodded his approval to the waiter, who applied his corkscrew to the bottle. "Not easy. Are you feeling creative?"

They had decided to eat in the hotel restaurant, which offered the local fish, the local white wine from Cassis, and a front-row view of the local sunset over the Vieux Port. It was still early, and apart from a table of businessmen taking their briefcases and marketing plans out for a festive dinner they had the restaurant to themselves.

"I've been thinking about it," said Sophie.

"If what Philippe says is true, to see Reboul is not a problem. We could say we were doing a profile of him for a magazine . . ." She stopped. Sam was already shaking his head.

"He'd want to know the name of the magazine, and his people would probably want to call the magazine editor to make sure it wasn't going to be a hatchet job. In any case, interviewing Reboul is just a smoke screen, the means to an end. It's really the cellar we want to see. The wines."

Sophie's experience of deceit and bluff was limited to the occasional socially delicate dinner party in Bordeaux, but she found she was enjoying the challenge of inventing a credible piece of fiction. "I know," she said. "You are a rich American who wants to make a wonderful cellar — in a hurry, of course, like all rich Americans — and I am your consultant. We come to Reboul for inspiration, because we have heard he has one of the best cellars in France."

Sam was frowning. "But what's in it for him? Why should he help two strangers?"

"Because he likes to be flattered." Sophie shrugged. "All men do — successful men most of all."

"Sure. But it's not enough of a reason, not for someone who loves publicity. And we know he loves publicity. He doesn't seem the kind of guy who does good deeds in secret."

Sam was about to pour the wine when he paused, the bottle halfway between the ice bucket and Sophie's glass. "What was that you said just now? About Reboul having one of the best cellars in France?"

Sophie nodded. "So?"

"You say 'best cellar' to me and I think of a book. You know, a best seller. Now, suppose we were putting together a book. A big, glossy, expensive book. A book that's all about the best cellars in France — no, make that the best cellars in the world — and we wanted to include Reboul's cellar." Sam was so taken up with his thoughts that he was oblivious to the dripping bottle in his hand and the patient waiter at his shoulder. "And why? Because it has everything: a great collection of wines, an extraordinary setting for a cellar, a fascinating and successful owner, everything. All of which, of course — and particularly the owner — would be photographed for the book by one of the world's top photographers. So Reboul would get his flattery, but it would be *public* flattery. And we'd have a reason to spend as long as we wanted in his cellar. Long enough to make notes. Long enough to take reference photographs." Sam sat back and gave up the bottle to the hovering waiter who had been waiting to fill their glasses. "What do you think?"

"Promising," said Sophie. "Actually, very good. But I have a big question. Who are we? I mean, which publishing company do we work for? Surely Reboul would want to know."

Sam found himself slipping into French ways, and gave Sophie a vigorous wag of his index finger. "We're not publishers. We're independent book packagers. We have an idea for a book. Let's say we call it *The World's Best Cellars.* Next, we commission people to write the text and take the photographs. We make up a dummy, and then we sell publishing rights to the highest bidder among the big international publishers. Bertelsmann, Hachette, Taschen, Phaidon — companies like that."

"How do you know all these things?"

Sam thought back to his one and only brush with the publishing business. "A couple of years ago, I happened to be on a job in Frankfurt during the book fair. It's a zoo, but it's a big deal — publishers from all over the world go there to buy and sell. I got to know a few of the publishing people who took over the hotel bar every night.

Boy, can those guys drink. They talked. I listened. I learned a lot. It was pretty interesting."

As Sophie and Sam made their slow and enjoyable way through sea bass with fennel, some fresh goat cheese with *tapénade,* and a rosemary sorbet, they bounced the idea back and forth, testing it for problems and adding a few embellishments. By the time coffee arrived, they felt they had a story that would stand up. In the morning, Sophie would get Reboul's office number from Philippe and, with luck, make an appointment. Sam would buy a camera and polish up their presentation.

"And I've just thought of the perfect way to end the evening," he said as he signed the check. "A moonlit snoop."

Sophie gave him a sideways look. "What is snoop?"

Sam tapped his nose and winked. "A clandestine reconnaissance. I thought it might be interesting to stroll up the road and take a look at our neighbor's house. Want to come?"

"Why not? I've never been on a snoop before."

Leaving the hotel, they turned up the hill and followed the Boulevard Charles Livon until they came to a pair of massive iron

135

gates, which had been left open. A driveway led up through the darkness toward a distant glow, presumably coming from the house.

"Now I've seen everything," said Sam. "A one-man gated community." He set off up the drive, a slightly nervous Sophie one step behind.

She tugged at his sleeve. "Sam? What do we say if someone stops us?"

"First, we stop whispering. Then we say — oh, I don't know, perhaps we're a couple of innocent American tourists and we thought this was a public park. But remember, we don't speak French. Smile a lot. You'll be fine."

As they moved farther up the driveway, the sound of traffic from the boulevard dropped to a muted rumble. Another two hundred yards found them at the end of a clipped lawn the size of a football field, and beyond it, ablaze with lights, the home of Francis Reboul.

Sam let out a soft whistle. "This place could give the White House an inferiority complex."

They stopped to take it in. The building in front of them at the far end of the lawn was colossal — a three-story, three-sided pile, with the two shorter sides enclosing a graveled forecourt. Almost lost in a corner of the forecourt were half a dozen black limousines parked in a precise row, and by the light streaming through the ground-floor windows they could see a knot of uniformed chauffeurs, chatting and smoking as they waited in the cool night air.

"Party time," said Sam. He looked at his watch. "We'd better not hang around. The guests may start coming out."

They were turning to leave when they were hit in the face by the beam of a powerful flashlight. A security guard and a German shepherd came out of the night toward them. Neither of them looked welcoming.

Sam could feel Sophie freeze beside him. He took a deep breath, held up his hands, and smiled into the glare. "Hi. We're kind of lost. Do you speak English?"

"Que faites-vous ici?"

"No, I guess you don't speak English."

The dog whined softly, and pulled his leash taut.

"We're looking for our hotel," said Sam. "The Sofitel. Hotel Sofitel?" He waved his arms, doing his best to seem like the kind of man who could lose one of the most conspicuous hotels in Marseille.

The guard came a little closer. He looked every bit as menacing as his dog. Sam

137

wondered if they took it in turns to bite. With a jerk of his head, the guard pointed the beam of his flashlight down the path. *"Au bout du chemin. Puis à gauche."*

"Gauche — that's left. Right? *Gracias* — no, wait — *merci."* Sam turned to Sophie. "I've had it with these goddamn languages. Next year we're going to Cape Cod."

The guard's scowl deepened, and he gestured again with his flashlight, as though trying to sweep them away with the beam. The dog's teeth gleamed in the light. Sophie took Sam's arm and started to steer him, still muttering, back down the driveway.

Safely back on the boulevard, Sophie breathed a sigh of relief and started to laugh. "Was that a good snoop? He was not at all *gentil,* that man."

"Poor guy," said Sam. "What a lousy job — walking around all night with a dog is enough to make anyone cranky. I wonder if he's a permanent fixture, or if he's just there for the guests. Judging by those chauffeurs, Reboul has some pretty fancy friends. And a pretty fancy house. I'm looking forward to taking a look at the inside."

They reached the hotel and picked up their keys at the desk. Sophie tried to stifle a yawn. It had been a long day, and Bordeaux seemed a long time ago.

"Are you all set for tomorrow?" asked Sam. "It could be your first day as a book packager. This is where it could get interesting."

"I've never met any book packagers. What do they wear?"

Sam grinned. "Something persuasive. Sleep tight. I'll see you in the morning."

"Bright and early?"

"Bright and early."

Sam stood under the shower and let his thoughts go back over the day. Philippe promised to be a great asset; he was helpful, had a good sense of humor, and was smart enough to see at once the possibilities of a scoop. Also, he gave the impression of being, as Sophie had said, slightly *louche*. There was a touch of the rogue about him. This was a quality that Sam had no problems identifying with, and he judged it to be a sound basis for a fruitful working relationship. Tomorrow would see if Philippe could deliver the goods on Reboul.

And then there was Sophie, who was altogether more complicated. Sam felt that she was to some extent a prisoner of her background — that very proper French bourgeois background, with its rules of social behavior and strictly observed table manners, its dress code, and its reluctance to embrace anything or anyone that didn't conform. Sophie might one day be different. She was intelligent, attractive, and a good sport, as she had shown by going with him that evening to the Palais du Pharo. She was in all respects a lovely woman. But, as Sam admitted to himself with a sigh, she wasn't Elena Morales.

He stepped out of the shower, wrapped a towel around his waist, and went through to the bedroom. His phone was on the night table next to his watch. He looked at the time. It was midafternoon in L.A., and Sam could imagine Elena, after one of those birdlike lunches at her desk, fending off more calls from Danny Roth and wondering what progress, if any, Sam had made. He was tempted to call. But what could he tell her? The truth? That he wanted to hear her voice? He told himself to wait until tomorrow, when there might be something solid to report.

He spent a mystifying half hour trying to follow a rugby game on French television, and fell asleep with the roar of the crowd in his ears.

THIRTEEN

Sam went out into the fresh morning air and inspected his breakfast. Neatly arranged on the crisp white cloth that covered the table on his terrace was everything a reasonable man could want at the start of the day: an aromatic pot of *café filtre,* a large jug of hot milk, two chubby golden croissants, and a copy of the *Herald Tribune.* He put on his sunglasses, checked that the view was still as fine as it had been yesterday, and sat down with a pleasant sense of well-being. His cell phone rang.

Before answering, he looked at his watch. Sophie was acquiring American habits. "Good morning," he said. "You're up early."

"Old men can't sleep, Sam. You'll find out." The voice was soft, and slightly accented. Axel Schroeder.

Sam took a moment to get over his surprise before answering. "This is a treat, Axel. Good to hear from you. What's happening?"

"Oh, this and that, Sam. This and that. I thought maybe we should have a drink tonight." There was a pause. "If you're still in Paris."

Fishing, Sam thought. You've probably already called the Montalembert and found that I left. "Nothing I'd like better, Axel. But tonight's not possible."

"That's a shame," said Axel. "I hate to give bad news over the phone." Sam could hear him sigh. "I'll make it quick. Without going into details, the word I hear is that Roth set up the wine job."

"Really?"

"Yes. I'm afraid you're wasting your time in France. You should be back in California. That's my advice."

"Thanks, Axel. I'll be sure to let you know how it goes."

Shaking his head, Sam poured his first cup of coffee. He liked Axel, and there were times when he could surprise you — and probably himself — by telling the truth. But not this time, Sam felt sure. It was an encouraging sign. He tore off the end of a croissant and dipped it in his coffee, another French habit he'd picked up; messy, but delicious. He felt the warmth of the sun on his shoulders, and turned to the sports section of the paper.

Eleven o'clock found Sophie, Sam, and Philippe sitting around a table in a quiet corner of the hotel lobby. Sophie had spent the first part of the morning negotiating her way through the protective layers of Reboul's entourage. She had finally managed to reach his private secretary, only to be told that Monsieur Reboul was with his power-yoga teacher and couldn't be disturbed. The secretary had promised to call back.

"What did you tell her?" asked Philippe.

Sophie went through the cover story, with Philippe nodding his approval as she described her new incarnation as a book packager.

"That might work," he said when she had finished. He then took a thick folder from his weather-stained nylon backpack. "*Voilà:* Reboul's file. I printed out the interesting stuff so you don't need a computer to read it. You'll see from this how he loves attention, and if there's a photograph involved he loves it even more. Just like a politician." He stopped and grimaced. "Well, maybe not that bad. Here, take a look." He opened the folder and started to spread the contents on the table.

There was Reboul the master builder in a

hard hat on one of his construction sites; Reboul the newspaper magnate, sleeves rolled up in what looked like a newsroom; Reboul in a soccer shirt, chatting to members of the Olympique de Marseille team; Reboul in a frayed straw hat, secateurs at the ready, communing with a bunch of grapes; Reboul the aviator about to board his private jet; Reboul the sea dog at the helm of his yacht; and, in a variety of outfits that ranged from a business suit to T-shirt and shorts, Reboul the proud homeowner, *chez lui* in the Palais du Pharo. One study of particular interest was Reboul the connoisseur, holding a glass of wine to the light in front of racks of bottles that stretched away into the far distance; this was presumably his cellar.

Sam half expected to come across pictures of Reboul in his pajamas, but perhaps the great man didn't have time for sleep. "Busy guy," said Sam. "Does he have his own personal photographer?"

Philippe grinned. "At least one. Editors who know him well sometimes don't even bother to send a photographer when they're doing a piece."

"How about a wife? Is there a Madame Reboul?"

"There was. She died years ago, and he

never remarried. That's not to say he doesn't have one or two *petites amies.*" Philippe shuffled through the articles until he found a photograph of Reboul and a striking young woman who was several inches taller than he was. "Little men with big wallets," said Philippe. "They're always the most frisky, and they always go for tall women. Isn't that right, Sophie?" He waggled his eyebrows at her.

She made a face, but before she could reply her phone rang. The two men watched as she got up and moved away to take the call. It was brief, and it was positive. There was a wide smile on Sophie's face as she came back to the table. "Six-thirty this evening," she said. "It has to be tonight, because he's taking his boat to Corsica tomorrow, and he'll be away for a few days."

"Terrific," said Sam. "Well done. You have a great future as a book packager. Now, what do we need for this evening? I'd better get a camera."

"I need to find an outfit," said Sophie. "Something businesslike."

Philippe looked at his watch. "I need lunch. In fact, I will perish without lunch," he said. "I know this place, *typiquement marseillais.* We can talk while we eat."

The taxi dropped them on the corner of

the Rue de Village, a side street off the Rue de Rome. Philippe led the way to what appeared to be an ordinary butcher's shop, its window decorated with a panorama of beef, lamb, and veal. He stopped short at the entrance and turned to Sam. "I hope you're not a vegetarian?" He answered his own question with a shake of his head. "I forget. You're American. Of course you love meat. And here we have the best meat in Marseille."

As they went through the door, Sam could hear the buzz of conversation drifting through from the back of the shop. A young man came out to greet them, survived a vigorous embrace from Philippe, and took them into a small, crowded room dappled with light filtering through the leaves of the giant bougainvillea that sprawled across the glass roof. Philippe was looking around, nodding and smiling at several of the other customers. "Everybody here is from Marseille," he said to Sam, with some satisfaction. "You're probably their first American." Sam had been studying the surroundings, which owed a substantial debt to the bovine school of interior decoration. Depictions of a large, stately, black-and-white cow named La Belle were everywhere, on paintings and place mats, salt cellars and pepper shakers and menus. "I guess we know what we're going to eat," said Sam. "Any special recommendations?"

Philippe closed his menu with a snap. "*Bresaola* to start, with hearts of artichoke, sun-dried tomatoes, and Parmesan. Then the beef cheeks, which they do here with a slice of *foie gras* on top. And a *fondant au chocolat.* That will see us through until dinner. Trust me."

As they were making their way through lunch, one perfect mouthful after another, Philippe turned his attentions to Sophie. It had been too long since they had seen one another, he felt, and he wanted to catch up. After one or two harmless questions about work and Bordeaux, he sipped his wine, wiped his lips on his napkin, and moved on to more delicate matters.

"How's your love life?"

"Philippe!" Sophie flushed prettily and appeared to find something fascinating on her plate.

"Well, I'm sure you're not still married to that — what was he? A yacht designer? I always thought there was something a bit *louche* about him." He paused, head tilted, and studied Sophie. "I'm right, aren't I?"

Sophie nodded. "The divorce has just come through."

"And?" said Philippe. "And?"

"And I've been seeing someone else for nearly eighteen months." She looked at Sam, shaking her head. "This is what you get when you have a journalist in the family." Turning back to Philippe, she said, "His name is Arnaud Rolland, he has a small château near Cissac, a sweet old mother, no children, and two Labradors. Now let me finish my lunch."

Philippe looked sideways at Sam and winked. "Just asking," he said.

Over coffee, the conversation returned to the events of the evening. "Before I forget," said Philippe as he rummaged in his backpack. "Your *devoirs* — something for you to read before tonight." He slid a small book across the table to Sam. "It's the story of the Palais du Pharo, actually very interesting. Reboul is proud of his home. You will impress him if you can show you know a little about it."

"Philippe?" Sophie was studying a street plan of Marseille. "Where would you go if you wanted to buy clothes?"

Philippe glanced down and brushed an imaginary speck of dust from the wrinkled, olive drab fatigue pants that were tucked into scuffed combat boots. "There's an army surplus place off the Canebière. I know the owner. He understands *mon 'look.'* "

"No, not for you. Me."

Philippe gazed at the ceiling in thought. "I'd say Rue Paradis, Rue Breteuil, the little streets around there. I'll mark them for you."

They stood outside the restaurant while Philippe pointed them in the direction of their destinations — Sophie for her boutiques, Sam for his camera. Philippe himself, shouldering the unforgiving burden of journalism, was off to cover the first-ever Salon d'Erotisme to be held in Marseille, a unique and perhaps largely unclothed event. As he speculated aloud on what he might see, Sophie put her hands to her ears and left.

Back once again on his terrace, Sam settled down and opened the book Philippe had given him, a slim volume in two languages that set out the history of what was now Reboul's splendid home.

The idea for the Palais du Pharo was conceived in 1852, when Louis-Napoléon, *le prince-président* on his way to becoming emperor, dropped a hint to the local dignitaries that a residence overlooking the sea might be very much to his liking.

A hint from Napoléon was not too far

from an imperial command, and the good people of Marseille were quick to respond. Let us build you a house, they said. Napoléon, thinking that their generosity was a little excessive (a sense of moderation not normally found in emperors), turned down the offer. But, he said, he would be delighted to accept a suitable plot of land, and on it he would construct a suitable house.

As sometimes happens in Provence, the building process was slow, and not without its problems. Although work officially commenced in 1856, the first stone wasn't laid until 1858, on August 15 — which, by happy coincidence, was Saint Napoléon's Day. It was one of very few happy moments. The numerous architects squabbled, the head mason was incompetent, there were not enough workmen assigned to the job, there were difficulties with the supply of stone, and frequent fierce winds demolished the windows. Work dragged on for another ten years, but as 1868 came and went Napoléon's *palais* was still uninhabitable.

Worse was to come. Two years later, after some injudicious military adventures, Napoléon was deposed. He went into exile in England, where he died in 1873. His widow, Eugénie, gave back to Marseille what had been given to her and her husband, leaving the city as the owner of the most spectacular white elephant on the coast.

Over the 120years that followed, the city fathers discovered that enormous houses, particularly those exposed to the ravages of salt sea air, cost enormous amounts of money to keep up. Dozens of schemes to defray costs were tried and discarded. Eventually, it was with a considerable sense of relief that the city accepted Reboul's offer to rent the Palais du Pharo for his personal use. Papers were signed on Saint Napoléon's Day 1993, and Reboul moved in.

It was a sad little story, Sam thought as he closed the book. If an emperor couldn't get a house built in ten years, what hope was there for the rest of us?

The early-evening breeze coming off the sea had turned chilly, and he went inside to change into a suit and tie for the meeting. He checked his new camera and put half a dozen business cards in his top pocket. These were printed only with his name and address. There were no details about his occupation, since this had a way of changing from job to job. With a final adjustment of his tie — a Harvard Club knockoff — he went down to meet Sophie in the lobby.

She was already there when Sam stepped out of the elevator, and she was talking to an extremely attentive concierge, who clearly appreciated what she was wearing. It was the Frenchwoman's version of a business suit — that is, a skirt just the modest side of short, with a hint of lacy *décolleté* visible beneath the fitted jacket.

When she saw Sam, Sophie turned toward him, one hand on her hip, her eyebrows raised. "So? Will this do?"

Sam nodded his head and grinned. "You're a credit to the publishing business. In fact, you'd be a sensation in the publishing business."

"I've just asked the concierge to call for a taxi," she said. "Twenty meters is about all I can manage in these shoes."

Sam looked at the shoes. It was his turn to raise his eyebrows. "I understand perfectly," he said. He offered Sophie his arm. "Let's go. This is Reboul's lucky night."

FOURTEEN

The iron gates swung open to let the taxi through. Standing some fifty meters inside the gates, at the very edge of the driveway, was a larger-than-life-size statue of a woman clad in the flowing robes of ancient Greece. Her blind marble gaze was fixed on the huge building in the distance, her arms outstretched as if trying to touch it.

The driver nodded toward her as they passed. "Empress Eugénie," he said. "*La pauvre.* This is about as close as she ever got to her palace."

Waiting on the front steps as the taxi pulled up was a young man in a dark suit, his head respectfully tilted in welcome. He guided them through the entrance and along a gleaming avenue of honey-colored herringbone parquet that led to a pair of tall double doors. These he threw open with a flourish before melting away, leaving Sophie and Sam almost blinded by the torrent of evening sunlight that streamed through a row of floor-to-ceiling windows. Framed by one of these windows was the silhouette of Reboul, his back to the room and a cell phone to his ear.

Sophie nudged Sam. "He doesn't know we're here."

"Sure he does," said Sam. "He's just letting us know how busy he is. They do it all the time in L.A." He turned, and closed the double doors behind him with a firm thump. The sound seemed to be enough to attract the silhouette's attention, and Reboul, still heavily backlit, put away his phone and came across to greet them.

He was short, slim, and immaculate. He had thick white hair, beautifully cut *en brosse,* and wore a shirt of the palest blue, a tie that Sam, a student of these arcane signals, recognized as the official neckwear of the Guards Club in London, and a dark-blue silk suit. His face was the color of oiled teak, and his bright brown eyes became even brighter at the sight of Sophie.

"Bienvenue, madame," he said, bending over to kiss her hand and take in her *décolleté* before turning to Sam. *"Et vous êtes Monsieur . . ."*

"Levitt. Sam Levitt. Good to meet you. Thanks a lot for seeing us." He shook Reboul's hand and gave him one of his business cards.

"Ah," said Reboul. "You would prefer that we speak English."

"That's kind of you," said Sam. "My French is not as good as it should be."

Reboul shrugged. "No problem. Today, everyone in business must know English. All my employees speak it. Soon, I suppose, We'll have to learn Chinese." He looked down at Sam's card, and cocked a bushy white eyebrow. "A château in Los Angeles? How chic."

"A modest place," said Sam with a smile. "But it's home."

Reboul extended a hand toward the row of windows. "Come. Let me show you my sunset. I'm told it's the best in Marseille."

His sunset, thought Sam. It was wonderful how billionaires had a habit of appropriating the marvels of nature as their personal property. But he had to admit that it was an exceptional sight. The sky was on fire — a great crimson gash, fading at the edges to tones of pink and lavender, the light making a path of rippled gold on the surface of the sea. Reboul nodded at the view, as if in confirmation that it was up to the normal high standard that he expected.

A few kilometers from the shore, there was

a shadowy huddle of small islands. Sophie pointed to the nearest of them. "That's the Château d'If, isn't it?"

"Quite right, my dear. You obviously haven't forgotten your Alexandre Dumas. This is where the Count of Monte-Cristo was imprisoned. Many visitors think he really existed, you know." He chuckled. "Such is the power of a good book." Turning away from the window, he took Sophie's arm. "Which reminds me of the reason for your visit. Let's sit down, and you can tell me about it."

Reboul showed them to a group of nineteenth-century chairs and sofas arranged around a low table that dripped with ormolu. Before sitting down himself, he took out his cell phone and pressed a button. The young man in a dark suit, who must have been lurking outside, appeared with a tray that he set down on the table. He took a bottle of champagne from its ice bucket and presented it for Reboul's approval before opening it. The cork came out with a gentle sigh. The young man poured, served, and disappeared.

"I hope you like Krug," said Reboul. He settled back in his chair and crossed his legs, exposing black crocodile loafers and a pair of trim, deeply tanned bare ankles. "You must forgive the lack of socks," he said, "but I detest them. I never wear them at home." He raised his glass to Sophie and smiled. "To literature."

When Sam and Sophie were planning their pitch, they had agreed that Sophie's Bordeaux background made her the natural choice for the part of editorial director, in charge of selecting the cellars to be included in the book. With a sip of champagne to moisten a suddenly dry throat, she started by giving Reboul a general overview of the project, sprinkling her explanation with names of the eminent professional cellars under consideration — the grand restaurants and hotels of the world, and, of course, the Elysée Palace. Reboul listened with polite attention, his eye occasionally wandering from Sophie's face to a discreet appreciation of her legs.

As she moved on to what she called the major part of the book — the world's finest private cellars — Reboul's interest increased. He asked who else besides himself would be approached. It was a question that Sophie had anticipated, and without hesitation she reeled off the names of a handful of English aristocrats, some well-known American industrialists, Hong Kong's richest man, a reclusive Scottish widow who lived in a castle on thirty thousand acres of the Highlands, and two or three of the better-known families in Bordeaux and Burgundy.

Sophie was warming to her task, and Reboul was clearly warming to Sophie as she leaned toward him to emphasize the point she was about to make. Candidates for the book, she said, had to satisfy three requirements. First, they had to be people with sufficient taste and money to have put together a truly remarkable collection of wines. Second, they had to be interesting for reasons other than their love of wine — people who had, in Sophie's words, a life beyond the cellar. And third, the cellars themselves had to be, in one way or another, out of the ordinary. She cited two examples of what she meant: the English earl who kept his wines in a towering Victorian folly, complete with humidity-controlled elevator, at the end of his garden; and the American who had put aside an entire floor of his Park Avenue triplex for his collection. Without having seen the cellars of the Palais du Pharo, she said, she couldn't imagine that they were anything short of extraordinary.

Reboul nodded. "Indeed they are. And quite large. In fact, Monsieur Vial, my cellar master, keeps a small bicycle down there to get from one end to the other." He raised a hand, and the young man materialized to refill their glasses. "It is an interesting project, and most charmingly explained." He inclined his head toward Sophie. "But tell me a little about the — how can I put it? — the nuts and bolts. How does one prepare such a book?"

It was Sam's turn. The very best people would be commissioned, he assured Reboul. The text would be assigned to an internationally respected wine writer — Hugh Johnson came to mind, obviously — perhaps with a foreword by Robert Parker; the photographs were to be taken by Halliwell or Duchamp, both of whom were generally regarded as masters. The overall appearance of the book would be supervised by Ettore Pozzuolo, a design genius and publishing legend. In other words, no expense would be spared. This was going to be nothing short of a bible for wine lovers. Here, Sam corrected himself. It would be *the* bible for wine lovers, and there were millions of these throughout the world. Naturally, said Sam, Reboul would be given full approval of the text and photographs used, with Madame Costes acting as the liaison between writer, photographer, and the Palais du Pharo. She

159

would at all times be available for consultation.

Reboul pulled at the lobe of one leathery ear as he thought. He was aware that he was being flattered, but that never worried him. It was, he thought, not a bad idea, not bad at all. It was the kind of book that he himself would find interesting. And as long as his right of content approval was written into an agreement, there could be no embarrassing surprises when the book was published. It would be yet another testament to his success — the tycoon with a palate of gold. And not least of the attractions was the prospect of many cozy editorial meetings with the enchanting Madame Costes, who was looking at him so hopefully.

He made up his mind. "Very well," he said. "I agree. Not for personal publicity, of course, but because I am always looking for opportunities to beat the drum for France and everything French. It's a hobby of mine. I suppose I'm an old-fashioned patriot." He paused to let this noble sentiment sink in before continuing. "Now then. As my secretary told you, I leave early tomorrow morning for a few days in Corsica. But you have no need of me at this stage. The man you should see is Monsieur Vial. He has been in charge of my cellar for almost thirty years. There are several thousand bottles, and I sometimes think he knows each one of them personally. There is nobody better to give you the guided tour." Reboul nodded, and said again, "Yes, Vial is the man you must see."

As he was speaking, Sophie's expression had turned from hope to delight. She leaned forward to put her hand on Reboul's arm. "Thank you," she said. "You won't regret it, I promise you."

Reboul patted her hand. "I'm sure I won't, my dear." He looked across at the ever-hovering young man. "Dominique will make the arrangements for you to meet Vial tomorrow. And now, if you'll excuse me, I have another appointment. Dominique will take you back to your hotel."

On their way out, they almost bumped into Reboul's next appointment, a tall, sleek girl wearing large, dark sunglasses — in case the sun should magically reappear for an encore — and leaving in her wake a drift of scent.

"Shalimar," said Sophie with a disapproving sniff, "and far too much of it."

Standing on the steps outside the entrance waiting for the car, Sam put his arm around Sophie's shoulder and squeezed. "You were sensational," he said. "I thought for a moment you were going to sit on his lap."

Sophie laughed. "I think he thought so too. He's quite the ladies' man." She pursed her lips. "Although perhaps a little short."

"Not a problem, believe me. If he stood on his wallet he'd be taller than both of us put together."

A long, gleaming black Peugeot pulled up in front of the steps, and Dominique leaped out to open the rear doors.

"Just down the road, please," said Sam. "The Sofitel."

As they reached the end of the drive, the car stopped next to the statue of Empress Eugénie. Dominique lowered his window, stretched out a hand, and pressed a button that was concealed in a fold of Eugénie's marble robes. The electric gates swung open. With a murmured *Merci, madame,* Dominique turned onto the boulevard, and, minutes later, they were back at the hotel.

"I don't know about you," said Sam to Sophie, as the car pulled away, "but I think we've earned another drink. I'll race you to the bar."

As they crossed the lobby, a large, disheveled figure hurried over to intercept them, his eyebrows raised, his shoulders hunched, his hands spread wide. A human semaphore, fresh from the Salon d'Erotisme.

"*Alors? Alors?* How did it go?"

Sam gave two thumbs up. "Sophie was fantastic. We've got a date to visit the cellar tomorrow morning. How about you? Did you have an erotic afternoon?"

The big man grinned. "You would be amazed. Many novelties — you should see what they do with latex nowadays. For instance —"

"Philippe! Enough." Sophie was shaking her head all the way to the bar.

Over drinks, they brought Philippe up to date. It had been a promising start, they all agreed, but tomorrow would be key, and there was a lot of ground to cover. From Reboul's description, his cellar was gigantic, a bicycle ride from one end to the other. Not only that. They would be looking for a mere five hundred bottles among thousands. It was going to be a long day.

Sam finished his drink and stood up. "I think I'd better go and make a few calls. The folks in L.A. will be wanting to know what's going on, and it's best to get them before lunch. But I'm sure you two have a lot of family gossip to catch up on."

Philippe looked disappointed. "Don't you want to hear about the Salon d'Erotisme?"

"With a passion," said Sam. "But not tonight."

It was eleven a.m. in Los Angeles, and Elena Morales was beginning to wonder if she might find any entries in the Yellow Pages under "Human Disposal." Danny Roth's calls — whether snide, abusive, or threatening — were getting her down to the extent that she was having frequent daydreams about arranging for his extermination. Added to that was her irritation at Sam's prolonged silence and the frustration of not knowing what, if any, progress was being made in France. And so when her secretary announced that Mr. Levitt was on the line, she was ready to bite his head off.

"Yes, Sam. What is it?" The tone of her voice was several degrees below freezing.

"One of the many things I love about you," said Sam, "is your telephone manner. Now listen."

It took him five minutes to go through all the events leading up to the meeting with Reboul and the next day's visit to his cellar. Elena let him finish before she spoke.

"So your underworld buddy Axel Schroeder told you that it was Roth who organized the robbery?"

"That's right."

"But you didn't believe him. And you don't know if this Reboul guy has the wine?"

"That's right."

"And if he does, how are you going to prove it?"

"I'm working on that." Silence from the other end. "Elena, you sound less than excited."

"I had the Paris office send over Sophie Costes' C.V."

"And?"

"There's a photograph. It's not exactly how you described her." Sam could almost feel the chill coming down the line. "Good night, Sam." The phone went dead before he had a chance to reply.

FIFTEEN

Sam was up early, still at odds with himself about the previous night's phone call. He should have called Elena back and explained. No, he shouldn't. To hell with it. If she wanted to jump to conclusions, let her jump. He paced up and down, feeling a strong sense of *déjà vu.* This was how their fights had often started in the old days: suspicion from her, pigheadedness from him. It had made for a stormy relationship — but, it must be said, for some spectacular reconciliations. He shrugged the memories away and turned his attention to the Reboul dossier that Philippe had left with him.

Sam's French was far from fluent, but as he plodded through the articles he managed to pick up the gist of much that had been written. One recurring theme — no matter what role Reboul was playing, whether newspaper czar or pirate of the Mediterranean — was the greatness of

France and all things French. Culture, language, cuisine, wines, châteaus, couture, French women, French soccer players, and on and on. Even the TGV high-speed trains, although Reboul admitted never actually having traveled on one, were given a ringing endorsement. And somehow he made it sound as though he had played a vital part in the creation of it all.

Reboul's only concession to the possibility that France might be less than an earthly paradise was his disdainful opinion of the *fonctionnaires,* that gray army of bureaucrats that infests every area of French life. Here was a hobbyhorse he mounted in public each spring when he gave his income-tax press conference, to mark what he called the *fête des fiscs,* or the festival of the tax man. Not content with simply telling the world how much tax he had paid, he translated the figure into its equivalent in *fonctionnaires'* salaries. This provided an appropriate starting point for his annual rant against the idleness, incompetence, and waste of the bureaucracy, which always went down extremely well with the popular press. But that was it — a single blot on the otherwise perfect French landscape.

Reboul was an oddity among billionaires. Most of them preferred to spend their lives ducking in and out of the havens of Nassau or Geneva or Monaco, on constant alert in case the tax laws should change. Sam couldn't help but like a man who was prepared to pay the price to live in the country he so obviously loved. With a nod of approval, he closed the file and went down to meet Sophie in the lobby.

Florian Vial was waiting for them in front of the main entrance to the Palais du Pharo. Had they not known that he was in charge of Reboul's cellar, they would have taken him for a professor, or perhaps a poet fallen on good times. Despite the mild spring temperature, he was dressed for the chill of the cellar in a suit of thick, bottle-green corduroy. Wrapped several times around his neck, in the complicated French fashion, was a long black scarf. A hint of plum-colored shirt showed beneath his jacket. His hair, worn long and brushed straight back, was the same mixture of salt and pepper as his beard, which had been clipped into a neat triangle. Pale-blue eyes peered out through round, rimless spectacles. There was a definite air of the nineteenth century about him. All he needed was an oversized fedora and a cloak, and he could have been a subject for Toulouse-Lautrec, a boulevardier on his way to pay a call on his mistress.

He bent over to kiss Sophie's hand, brushing her fingers with his whiskers. *"Enchanté, madame. Enchanté."* Turning to Sam, he shook hands with a vigorous pumping motion. *"Très heureux, monsieur,"* he said, and then stepped back, raising both hands in the air. *"Mais pardonnez-moi.* I forget. Monsieur Reboul tells me that you prefer English. This is no problem for me. My English is fluid." His eyes twinkling, he beamed at Sophie and Sam. "Shall we commence?"

With Vial leading the way, they went through a series of ornate rooms — Vial described them as *salons* — until they came to a vast kitchen. Unlike the *salons,* which had been allowed to retain their rather pompous period décor of chandeliers and gilt and swags and tassels, the kitchen was a study in modernity: stainless steel, polished granite, and recessed lighting. The only hint of bygone culinary tradition was an overhead cast-iron rack that held thirty or forty polished copper pans. Vial waved at the massive stove — a Le Cornu, with enough burners, hot plates, and ovens to service a banquet — and said, with considerable satisfaction, "The chef at Passédat, who is a friend of the *patron,* comes here often. He would kill to have such a kitchen."

They passed through to a second, less glamorous kitchen, a large room lined with storage closets, deep freezes, and dishwashers. In the corner were two doors. Vial opened the larger of the two and looked back over his shoulder. "The stairs are very narrow. *Attention!* As you say — slowly does it."

The stairs were not only narrow, but steep, and wound around in a tight spiral before coming to an end in front of a door of painted steel. Vial pressed some numbers on the electronic keypad that was set into the wall and opened the door. Turning on the lights, he stood aside to watch the reaction of his guests, a smile on his face. This was obviously a moment he relished.

Sophie and Sam stayed rooted to the threshold, stunned into silence. Stretching away in front of them for a good two hundred yards was a broad, flagstone passageway with a barely perceptible downward slope. The ceiling was a series of lofty, graceful vaults constructed of old brickwork that the effects of time had softened to a pale, dusty pink. Leading off on either side were smaller passages, their entrances marked by square, head-high brick columns. To the left of the door, propped against a barrel, was

Vial's bicycle, an elderly Solex. The air smelled as the air in a cellar should smell: faintly humid, faintly musty.

Vial was the first to break the silence. "*Alors?* What do you think? Will it fit into your book?" He was smiling as he stroked his moustache with the back of an index finger, the picture of a man who knows that he is about to receive a compliment.

"Very, very impressive," said Sophie. "Even in Bordeaux, one would never find a cellar this large, not in a private house. It's magnificent, Sam, don't you think?"

"Perfect," said Sam. "Just great for the book." He grinned at Vial. "The only problem is you need a map to find your way around."

Vial almost burst with self-satisfaction. "But of course I have such a map! *Mais oui!* We must go down to my office, and I will show you how to get as you say from A to B."

They set off down the flagstone pathway, with Vial settling into his role as tour guide. "Here everything is streets, you know, like in a town. We are actually on the main street." He pointed out a small blue and white enamel sign, placed at eye level on the first column they came to, marked Boulevard du Palais. "And off to each side,"

171

Vial continued, "are other streets, some big, some small." He stopped and raised a finger. "But the name of each street tells us who lives there." A wag of the finger. "I speak of bottles, of course." He beckoned them off to the side and into one of the passages. Another blue and white sign announced this as the Rue de Champagne.

And there it was, champagne in glorious abundance, filling racks on either side of a narrow gravel pathway: Krug, Roederer, Bollinger, Perrier-Jouët, Clicquot, Dom Pérignon, Taittinger, Ruinart — in bottles, magnums, Jeroboams, Rehoboams, Methuselahs, and even Nebuchadnezzars. Vial gazed at the display with the fondness of a doting parent before leading them out and down to the next street, the Rue de Meursault, followed in quick succession by the Rue de Montrachet, the Rue de Corton-Charlemagne, the Avenue de Chablis, the Allée de Pouilly-Fuissé, and the Impasse d'Yquem. This side of the main boulevard, Vial explained, was devoted to white wine; the opposite side to reds.

It took them almost an hour to travel the length of the cellar, stopping as they did to pay their respects here and there — to the great red Burgundies, for instance, in the Rue du Côte d'Or, and the legendary trio of Latour, Lafite, and Margaux in the Rue des Merveilles. By the time they had reached Vial's office they felt curiously light-headed, as if they had been tasting rather than just looking.

"Let me ask you a question," said Sam. "I didn't see a Rue de Chianti. Do you have any Italian wines?"

Vial looked at Sam as though he had insulted his mother. When he'd finished shaking his head and clicking his tongue, he allowed himself to speak. "No, no, no, absolutely not. Every bottle here is French, as Monsieur Reboul has insisted. Only the best. Although . . ." Vial seemed of two minds about what he was going to say. "*Entre nous,* and not for the book, over there you will see a few cases from your California. Monsieur Reboul has a winery, as you say, in the Valley of Napa. He amuses himself. It's a hobby." And, judging from Vial's expression, not a hobby that he viewed with great enthusiasm.

At the very end of the cellar, a patriotic golf cart, painted in the blue, white, and red of the French *tricolore,* was parked in a corner, next to a giant pair of doors. At the touch of a button, these swung open to reveal the long driveway that led down to Eugénie's wistful statue and the gates to the property.

"You see?" said Vial. "The cellar is underneath *la grande pelouse,* the lawn in front of the house." He nodded at the cobblestoned area outside the doors. "This is for deliveries. The truck unloads here, into my *chariot de golf,* and I drive the bottles to their addresses."

Sophie looked at the golf cart with a frown on her face. "But Monsieur Vial, when you're ready to drink the wine, how does it get into the house? Not up those stairs, surely? Or do you drive your cart around . . ."

"Aha!" Vial tapped his nose. "Trust a woman to be practical. I will show you before we leave. Now we go to my office, and you will see my crazy furnishings."

It was becoming apparent that Vial saw a major supporting role for himself in the book, and he was at pains to point out the many objects of interest in his cluttered office. A colossal corkscrew, easily a meter long, with a handle made from a twisted, highly polished billet of olive wood, leaned against the wall by the side of his desk; a connoisseur's desk, Vial called it. Apart from the glass top, it had been constructed entirely out of wooden wine crates from the great estates, each crate used as a desk drawer, each drawer identified by the name and mark of an illustrious château stamped into the wood. The unobtrusive drawer handles were circular plugs of wood, stained to resemble corks.

Sam took out his camera and held it up. "Is it OK? Just for reference."

"But of course!" Vial moved across so that he would be in the shot, placed one hand on the desktop, raised his head and assumed a noble expression: the eminent *caviste,* caught during a rare moment of reflection.

Sam grinned at him. "You've done this before."

Vial flicked at his moustache and assumed a different pose, this time perching on the edge of the desk, his arms folded. "For wine magazines, yes. They always like what they call the human interest."

While Sam was taking pictures, Sophie studied the other examples of human interest that covered most of one wall: framed photographs of Vial with movie actors, soccer players, pop stars, fashion designers and models, and other distinguished visitors. These shared wall space with certificates from the Jurade de Saint-Emilion and the Chevaliers du Tastevin, and, in a suitably prominent position, a letter of thanks and appreciation from the Elysée Palace, signed by the President of the Republic himself. Like his boss Reboul, it seemed that Vial was not averse to a little self-promotion.

Moving away from the rogues' gallery, Sophie stopped at a long, wide shelf filled with alcoholic antiques — unopened bottles from the 1800s, their labels blotched and faded, their contents murky and mysterious. Her eye was caught by a bottle of what had once been white Bordeaux, an 1896 Gradignan, the remains of the wine resting on a five-inch layer of sediment. Vial tore himself away from the camera and brought Sam over to join her.

"My sentimental corner," he said. "I find these bottles at flea markets and I cannot resist them. Undrinkable, of course, but very picturesque, don't you think?"

"Fascinating," said Sophie. "And that, too." She pointed to a small copper alembic — the apparatus that distills grape sludge into *eau-de-vie* — standing in the corner. "Look at that, Sam. Do you have those in California?"

Sam shook his head. "Only for show. Does this one still work?"

Vial pretended to be shocked at the very idea. "Do I look like a criminal, monsieur? Not since, let me see, 1916, has it been allowed for private persons to distill their own, as you say, moonshine." He permitted himself a wink and a pleased smirk at having come up with such an appropriate foreign word. "And now, let me show you how to find your way around my little city." He walked back and waved an arm at the map that hung on the wall behind his desk.

It was perhaps eighteen inches high and three feet wide, a hand-drawn bird's-eye view of the cellar, with the street names marked in immaculate copperplate script. Surrounding the map, just inside the simple gilt frame, was a border of colorful miniature corkscrews, each with a different handle. Some were whimsical — a heart, a dog, a French flag, a bird's beak — others were the artist's version of more conventional models. The map had been signed in one corner and dated in Roman numerals.

"That's great," said Sam. "It would make terrific endpapers."

Sophie, who had no idea what he was talking about, nodded sagely. "Good idea."

Sam explained to a puzzled Vial that some books — the more elaborate and expensive editions — often had designs decorating their inside front and back covers. "Your map is a natural for a wine book," he said, "with all those names and corkscrews. You don't happen to have copies of it, do you?"

With another wink, Vial darted over to his desk, opened one of the bottom drawers, and produced a scroll, which he spread out on the desk for them to see. "These were printed before we framed the original. We give them as little souvenirs to the friends of Monsieur Reboul who come to the cellar for tastings. *Charmant, non?*" He rolled up the map and handed it to Sophie.

Vial cut short their thanks by looking at his watch and grimacing. "*Peuchère!* Where has the morning gone? I have a rendezvous in Marseille." He shepherded them from the office. "You must come back after lunch."

He climbed into the golf cart, motioning Sophie and Sam to follow. "Imagine you are a case of wine," he said to Sam, "and that tonight is your moment of glory, your night to flabbergast the guests of Monsieur Reboul, your night to be consumed with cries of ecstasy." He started the cart and set off up the Boulevard du Palais.

"Sounds like fun," said Sam. "Am I a case of red or a case of white?"

"Either," said Vial, "or both. It doesn't matter. The important problem for you is how to get up to the dining room." Arriving at the end of the boulevard, he parked the cart in front of the cellar door. "As you see," he said, getting out of the cart, "there is another door just here." He pointed to a low, narrow doorway set into the wall. With the air of a magician who has found not one but two white rabbits in his hat, he pulled open the door and stepped back. "*Voilà!* The elevator for bottles. It goes up to the back kitchen. There is no turbulence. There is no giddy feelings from climbing up the stairs. The wine arrives composed, relaxed, ready to meet its destiny."

"It's what we call a dumbwaiter," said Sam.

"Exactly," said Vial, mentally adding another colloquialism to his repertoire. "A dumbwaiter." He looked again at his watch, and flinched. "Shall we say three o'clock? I will meet you at the delivery door. And I give you a good address on the Vieux Port for lunch."

Sophie and Sam exchanged glances. *"Typiquement marseillais?"* said Sophie.

"Mais non, chère madame. A sushi bar."

SIXTEEN

They decided to forgo the pleasures of the sushi bar, which turned out to be a dim, crowded room on a side street, for sunshine and a sandwich on the terrace of La Samaritaine, across the road from the port. By the time a carafe of *rosé* and two *jambons beurres* had arrived, they were beginning to feel warm again after their subterranean morning among the bottles.

It had been an interesting visit. Vial, although rather too much of the showman for Sophie's conservative, Bordeaux-bred taste, ran a first-class cellar, beautifully organized and cobweb-free. And he couldn't have been more helpful. But, as they agreed, he had shown signs of being a little too helpful. Like an oversolicitous waiter, he had never left them alone. He'd been looking over their shoulders, going into raptures about this vineyard or that vintage, and generally being a well-intentioned distraction. It was a problem that needed to be dealt with. Identifying five hundred bottles among many thousands could take several hours and considerable concentration. An afternoon might do it, and they had the map to guide them. Even so, it wouldn't be easy, and Vial's hovering presence wouldn't help.

Sam poured two glasses of wine. A deeper color than the pale *rosés* that were currently fashionable in L.A., it almost matched the pink of the smoked ham in his sandwich. He raised his glass to the sun, took a sip, and held the wine in his mouth. A taste of summer. After a morning spent mingling with the wine aristocracy, it made a refreshing change to drink something simple, humble, but good — no long pedigree, no historic vintage, no complications, and no wildly inflated price tag. No wonder it was the favorite tipple of Provence.

"You know what?" he said. "When we go back this afternoon, it might be a good idea if we separated. One of us can stay on the white side, the other can check the reds. Vial can't be in two places at once. What do you think?"

Sophie thought for a moment, then nodded. "Let me take the whites."

"Sure. Any particular reason?"

"Most of the wines you're looking for are

red. You don't want Vial watching while you make notes or take pictures. Another thing — I'm from Bordeaux. I know about reds. Champagne and white Burgundy, not so much. So it is normal for me to ask Vial to explain them. He likes to talk, to show what he knows. You saw that this morning. I'm sure I only need to give him this much encouragement" — she held up her finger and thumb, a fraction of an inch apart — "and he'll talk to me all afternoon. *C'est certain.*" She was smiling as she looked at Sam over the top of her sunglasses.

"You're enjoying this, aren't you?"

"In one way, very much. It's a lot more amusing than insurance. Just like a game." She shrugged. "But I'm not sure I want us to win. Do you know what I mean?"

Sam knew exactly. Two or three times in the past, he'd been involved in cases where, for one reason or another, his sympathies lay with the criminal. "Yes, I know what you mean. Reboul and Vial seem like good guys." He grinned. "But then, good guys can be crooks. Look at me. I used to be one."

Sophie took in this revelation with no more surprise than if Sam had just told her he once played pro football. He was, after all, American, and anything was possible.

"Do you miss it — being a crook?"

"Sometimes." Sam sat back in his chair and watched an old man as he shuffled slowly across the road, threatening the oncoming traffic with his stick. "When you're on a caper, you're very aware of being alive. Intensely alive. I guess that's the risk, and the adrenaline. And I used to love the planning side of it, putting together a nice clean job: organized down to the last second, properly carried out. No guns, no violence, nobody gets hurt."

"Except the poor insurance company."

"Yeah, right. Show me a poor insurance company, and I'll show you proof that Santa Claus is alive and well and living in Florida. But I get what you're saying. There's always a victim." He thought of Danny Roth, but failed to summon up even a twinge of pity.

Sophie called Philippe to bring him up to date, and then they lingered over the last of the wine and some ferocious jolts of coffee until it was time to head back to the Palais du Pharo. This was it. By the end of the afternoon, they would know that they'd either been wasting their time or that they might be on their way to solving a classic long-distance crime, robbery *sans frontières.* Not only neat, but endearingly old-fashioned, a throwback to simpler times,

183

before theft was conducted using the marvels of electronics or the twisted talents of lawyers. As they stood in the sun waiting for a taxi, Sam checked his pockets: map, camera, spare battery, notebook, and the list of stolen wines. Five minutes to three. They were all set.

"And how was the sushi?" Vial didn't wait for an answer to his question before bustling them into his office. "I have arranged to liberate myself for the entire afternoon. *Je suis à vous.*" He cocked his head expectantly, and Sophie saw her chance.

"There's so much to see," she said, "so very much to see, that we thought it would be best if we each looked at half the cellar. I chose the whites, but with one condition." She gazed at Vial, and for one long moment Sam thought she was actually going to flutter her eyelashes. "Coming from Bordeaux, I am quite familiar with the great reds. However, the great champagnes, the great whites of Burgundy and Sauternes — although I know them by name, of course — are, how can I say, a gap in my education. And so I was hoping that you would . . ." Her voice tailed off, and her eyes remained fixed on Vial, who instinctively straightened his shoulders and raised a hand to stroke his moustache.

"My dear madame, nothing gives me greater pleasure than sharing what few scraps of knowledge I have with a fellow enthusiast." He started to move toward the door, a man with a mission. "I propose that we start with champagne and end with Yquem, as one would at a civilized dinner." Sam had the feeling that this was a line Professor Vial had used on his guided tours many times before.

They were passing through the doorway when Vial stopped suddenly, and turned to Sam. "But I forget my other guest. You will not be lonely? You will not lose yourself? You are sure?"

"I have your excellent map, I'll have some pretty good bottles to keep me company, and I don't mind working alone. Don't worry about me. I'll be fine."

Vial needed no persuading. "*Bon.* Now, dear madame, if you'd like to follow me, we will plunge at once into the champagnes. You will have heard, I'm sure, that champagne was invented by the monk Dom Pérignon, who said when he tasted his divine invention, 'I am drinking stars.' Never has there been a better description. He lived to a good age — seventy-seven, I believe, which is a testament to the medicinal qualities of champagne. What is less well known is the unusual relationship of the good monk with one of the neighboring nuns . . ." As he led Sophie away, his voice rose and fell, but never ceased. She had been right: Vial loved to talk, and he loved a pretty audience.

In the end, Sam's search was accomplished with far less time and difficulty than he had anticipated. The map of the cellar, an enormously helpful shortcut, led him first to the Rue des Merveilles: '53 Lafite, '61 Latour, '83 Margaux. All these vintages were present in impressive quantities, the years marked in chalk on the small slate tickets that identified each bin, or storage compartment. Vial was safely out of the way; Sam could barely hear his voice in the distance. He took a bottle of Lafite from its resting place and laid it carefully on the gravel floor, label uppermost. Crouching over the bottle, he photographed it, checking the shot to make sure that both name and date were legible before he replaced the bottle. He did the same again with the Latour, and again with the Margaux. So far so good.

He consulted the map, looking for the Rue Saint-Emilion. There it was, next to Pomerol, reflecting the actual geography of the vineyards. There was plenty of the '82 Figeac. Indeed, there was plenty of everything, wherever he looked, and he wondered how anyone could possibly drink it all before departing for the great cellar in the sky. Perhaps there were some thirsty little Rebouls lining up to inherit. Sam hoped so. It would be sad to see this magnificent collection broken up and consigned to the auction rooms.

He moved next door, to the Pomerols. One of the lower bins was devoted to magnums of the 1970 Château Pétrus. He counted them: twenty, a relatively modest number by Reboul standards. Using both hands, one on the capsule and one on the base, Sam took a magnum and laid it on the gravel, admiring as he did so the ornate design that occupied the top of the label. The artist had among the vine tendrils nestled a small portrait of Saint Peter with his key — the key to heaven. Or, as some like to say, the key to the château's cellar.

The photograph taken, Sam returned the magnum to its bin with some reluctance; mixed, however, with satisfaction. He had found — and had proof of finding — all the reds on his list. The one wine that remained was the '75 Yquem, which would be on the opposite side of the cellar.

He made his way back to the central boulevard and tried to establish how far Sophie and Vial had traveled from their first stop among the champagnes. As far as he could judge from the volume of Vial's dissertation, they were still somewhere in the rolling hills between Corton-Charlemagne and Chablis. Yquem would be last on the list. He had time.

Feeling an irrational sense that he was trespassing, he crossed over to the Impasse d'Yquem, the final section of the cellar before Vial's office.

As Sam had discovered when doing his homework, Château d'Yquem is often described as the world's most expensive wine. During its long history, it has attracted admirers as varied as Thomas Jefferson, Napoléon, the czars of Russia, Stalin, Ronald Reagan, and Prince Charles, all of them drawn to the wine's luminous golden complexion and its luscious, creamy taste. Fewer than eighty thousand bottles are produced each year, no more than a fraction of a drop of Bordeaux's annual production. And it keeps well. A bottle of the 1784vintage was opened, drunk, and pronounced by a group of fortunate connoisseurs to be perfect two hundred years later.

Reboul's collection of Yquems was perhaps the most impressive part of a dazzling cellar — not for its size, which was no more than a hundred bottles, but for the range of vintages. Some of the great years were there, starting with the 1937 and moving on to the '45, the '49, the '55, and the '67 before ending with the youngest, the '75. Sam selected a bottle, photographed it, and had just put it back with the other '75s when he froze. Vial's voice sounded uncomfortably close.

"Chablis, of course, is one of the best-known white wines in the world. But there is Chablis and there is Chablis."

"Ah bon?" said Sophie, who managed to imbue those two syllables with fascinated surprise.

"*Mais oui.* Now what we have here are the best, the *grands crus,* the wines that come from the hills to the north of the town. For instance, this Les Preuses." Sam could hear the sound of a bottle being slid out of its bin. "In the glass, this has the most ravishing color, gold, with perhaps the most delicate *soupçon* of green." The bottle slid back into its bin. Another was taken out. Holding his breath, Sam tiptoed out of the Impasse d'Yquem and returned to the other side of the boulevard, to the safety of the reds. And there he was discovered by Vial

189

and Sophie fifteen minutes later, studying the bins of Pomerol, camera back in his pocket and notebook in hand.

"Aha!" said Vial. "There he is, your colleague, hard at work. A busy bee, *non?* I hope he has found something to interest him?"

"Fabulous," said Sam. "Absolutely fabulous. A quite extraordinary collection."

"But you should see the whites," said Sophie. "The Burgundies! The Yquem! Monsieur Vial has given me the education of a lifetime."

Vial preened.

"I can't wait to see them," said Sam. "But I feel we've taken up too much of Monsieur Vial's time already today. Can I ask a big favor? Can we come back?"

"Of course." Vial fished in his pocket and brought out a card. "Here is the number of my *portable.* Oh, I remind myself — Monsieur Reboul called from Corsica to make sure you have everything you need."

After a prolonged exchange of effusive thanks from Sophie and Sam and charmingly modest disclaimers from Vial, they left the twilight of the cellar and emerged blinking into the late-afternoon sun.

They said little on their way back to the hotel, both digesting what they had seen during the past two and a half hours.

"Philippe said he'd meet us here," Sophie said as they came to the hotel driveway. "He can't wait to hear what we found. He says it's like a *roman policier* — you know, a police story."

Sam stopped abruptly. "Does he have any contacts with the police down here? Solid contacts? Cops he meets for a drink now and then?"

"I'm sure. They all do, the journalists. Look, he's here already." She pointed to Philippe's black scooter, half-hidden in the shrubbery that lined the drive. "Why do you ask about the police?"

"It's just a thought, but I'm beginning to feel we may need them."

SEVENTEEN

Philippe was on the phone, pacing around the lobby, his free hand going back and forth, up and down, side to side, as if conducting an invisible symphony orchestra. He was dressed, as usual, in military hand-me-downs, the pride of place going to a vintage combat jacket with hell on wheels stenciled across the back in dripping, blood-red capital letters. Seeing Sophie and Sam, he terminated his call with an instant dismissal, barely having time to mutter *"Au'voir"* before the phone was back in his pocket. Sam had often noticed that the French, who like nothing better than to talk, have a brusque, almost brutal way of ending their phone conversations. No lingering farewells for them; odd, for such a loquacious race.

"Alors? Alors?" Philippe was feverish with curiosity, and after kissing Sophie with a perfunctory peck on each cheek, turned to

Sam. "What did you find?"

"Plenty," said Sam. "I'll explain everything, but first I need to get some stuff from my room. Can you find us a table in the bar? I won't be long."

When he joined them five minutes later, it was with an armful of papers — his notes, Reboul's dossier, and a slim folder with material he'd brought over from L.A. He dropped everything on the table and placed his camera on top of the pile.

Philippe had put himself in charge of refreshments. "Sophie tells me you like *rosé*," he said, taking a bottle of Tavel from the ice bucket and filling their glasses. "*Voilà,* Domaine de la Mordorée." He made a bouquet out of his fingertips and kissed them. "Don't let it stop you talking."

"Thanks. OK, We'll take the good news first: we were looking for six wines from specific years, and I've seen them. They're all there, and thanks to Sophie I was able to get photographs of them." Sam tapped the camera. "But don't get too excited. It *is* good news, but it's nothing more than a start. The problem is that there were more than a hundred thousand bottles produced of each of the wines, except Yquem. And even there, production was around eighty thousand. So there's no shortage of wine around from those vintages, and Reboul's bottles could have been picked up quite legitimately over the years. OK? Now, if Vial keeps his records as well as he keeps the cellar, there should be receipts for everything. But that's where we have another problem: we can't ask to see those receipts without giving the game away. Also, we should never forget that Reboul didn't get rich by being stupid. If he's our guy, you can bet your life he will have organized dummy paperwork to hide behind, something that would give him the chance of saying he bought the wine in good faith. Liechtenstein, Nassau, Hong Kong, the Caymans — he could have gone through any of them. There are thousands of funny little companies around the world that can provide any documentation you want, for a fee. Then they disappear. Tracing them can take years. Ask the IRS." Sam stopped to taste his wine.

Philippe seemed to visibly deflate. "So that's the end of it," he said, with a sigh. "No story."

"It's not over yet," said Sam, and now he was smiling. "Something's been bugging me all day, and I just remembered what it is." He sorted through the papers in front of him and pulled out a photocopy. "This is the article in the *L.A. Times* about Roth's wine collection. It was picked up by the *Herald Tribune,* which has an international circulation. So wine buffs all over the world — including our friend Reboul — could have seen it." He pointed to the main photograph, a little blurred but reasonably distinct. "Now, there's Roth. See what he's holding?"

Philippe peered at the picture. "Pétrus. Looks like a magnum."

"That's right. Can you make out the date on the label?"

Philippe picked up the photocopy for a closer look. "Nineteen seventy?"

"Right again. It's one of the bottles that were stolen, and Roth is holding on to it for dear life with both hands. His prints will be all over it. Now here's the thing about fingerprints: they keep best in a humid environment, and the humidity level in a professional cellar like Reboul's will be around eighty percent. Perfect. In those conditions, prints on glass can last for years. Let's assume we're going to be lucky, and that nobody's thought to wipe every bottle. If Roth's prints are on some of the magnums in Reboul's cellar, I would argue that's evidence of theft."

There was silence around the table while

this had time to sink in.

"Sam, there's something else." Sophie was searching through Reboul's dossier. She pulled out a picture that showed him posing in front of his private jet. "I thought of it while I was looking at all those bottles with Vial. If you wanted to move a lot of wine from California to Marseille without using shippers, wouldn't it be, well, convenient, to have your own plane?"

Sam shook his head, irritated with himself at missing something obvious. "Of course. Private jets tend to get V.I.P. treatment. Limited formalities going out of the States, and probably none for the local hero coming back into Marseille." He grinned at Sophie. "You're getting good at this. Can you see the registration number?"

The three of them took a closer look at the photograph. Reboul was in the foreground, his arms folded, looking serious and businesslike in a dark suit, an industrial titan ready to girdle the earth. Behind him was his jet, sleek and white, with groupe reboulin large black letters running along the fuselage, and what looked like a streamlined version of the French flag painted on the tail. The shot had been composed, either by design or by accident, so that any sign of the plane's registration was hidden by Reboul's body.

"I guess that doesn't matter too much," said Sam. "The company name is probably enough."

"Enough for what?" Philippe had recovered his spirits, and was perched on the edge of his chair, leaning forward, his combat boots performing a soft tap-dance on the floor.

"Any jet using U.S. airspace has to file a flight plan — departure time, destination, estimated time of arrival. The details will be on a computer. I'm pretty sure the company name will be on there too." He looked at his watch: just after six p.m. in Marseille, nine a.m. in California. "There's someone in L.A. who might be able to help us. I'll see if he's there." Sam got up, looking for a quiet corner to make the call. "Philippe, while I'm gone, will you think about all the cops you know in Marseille? Friendly cops? We're going to need one."

Lieutenant Bookman picked up his phone and grunted into it — an ill-humored, dyspeptic grunt, prompted by too much coffee, too much work, and not enough sleep.

"Sounding good, Booky. How are you?"

"I'm feeling like I sound. Where the hell are you?"

"Marseille. Listen, Booky, I need a big favor. Well, two big favors."

A resigned sigh. "And I thought you were going to ask me to come over for lunch. OK, what do you want?"

"First, a complete set of Danny Roth's fingerprints. I may have found his wine, but I need proof. Do you have a guy free who could get over to his office today?"

"For Danny Roth? Are you kidding? They won't exactly be lining up to volunteer, but I'll see what I can do. Next?"

"Not quite so easy. I need to know if a private jet belonging to the Groupe Reboul left the Los Angeles area between Christmas Eve and New Year's Eve of last year."

"And? Type of jet? Registration? Point of departure?"

"Well, here's the problem. I don't have the registration, and I don't know which airport it could have left from. But my guess is that it won't be far from L.A."

"Great. That's a real help. Last time I looked, there were nine hundred and seventy-four airports of various sizes in California. And you want me to tell you if a private aircraft with no known registration left one of these nine hundred and seventy-four airports during a seven-day period? You want the pilot's golf handicap and next of kin while we're at it? How about his blood type?"

"Booky, you love a challenge. You know you do. And I'm prepared to offer an inducement. When I get back, We'll go up to Yountville and have dinner at the French Laundry. *Foie gras au torchon,* my friend. Venison chops. The works — and any wine on the list. Your choice, my treat."

There was a silent, thoughtful moment during which Sam could almost hear, very faintly, the sound of Bookman's taste buds quivering to attention. "Let me get this straight," said the lieutenant. "Are you attempting to bribe a member of the Los Angeles Police Department?"

"Guess so."

"That's what I thought. OK, give me whatever details you can about the plane, and the address where you're staying. I'll FedEx the prints and anything else I can find. Do I assume it's urgent? Dumb question. Everything's urgent."

Walking back to rejoin the others in the bar, his mind racing, Sam felt the familiar tingle of excitement and impatience that he always felt when jobs started to get interesting. The next step would depend on Philippe, and there was no doubt he was keen to help.

199

But did he have the contacts? And would he be able to twist the necessary arms?

Sam gave them a thumbs-up as he got back to the table. "With a bit of luck, we should have Roth's prints by tomorrow morning, and maybe something on Reboul's plane." He sat down and reached for his glass. "This is where you come in, Philippe. This is where you earn your scoop." Philippe made an effort to look suitably stern and determined. Sam took a long sip of wine before continuing. "What we have to do next is to check the magnums of Pétrus for prints. It won't take long, no more than an hour or so, but I can't do it. If it's going to be used as evidence, it needs to be done by a pro. Which means the police." He looked at Philippe, his eyebrows raised. "And we need to get the print expert in and out of the cellar without causing any suspicion. In other words, without Vial knowing. If he smells a rat, we might as well pack up and go home."

Philippe had been fidgeting in his chair, waiting for his turn to speak. "We might be lucky with the police," he said. "I have a contact, going back a few years now." He squinted into the distance, pushing a hand through his hair. "It was when I was taking a look at some of the rackets operated by the Union Corse. They're the boys from Corsica, a local version of the Mafia. The paper likes to keep an eye on them from time to time. Anyway, they weren't doing anything out of the ordinary, just the usual stuff: drugs, illegal immigrants from North Africa, extortion down at the docks, protection in the city, that kind of thing.

"In those days there was a club where a lot of them used to go to throw their money around and impress the girls. And it wasn't just money they threw around. There was plenty of coke and heroin, too." He stopped to take a copious swig of wine.

"One of the girls — very sweet, very innocent — fell for the wrong guy. He got her on heroin. I often used to see her in the club, and she was a mess. And what made it worse was the way he treated her." He made a face and shook his head. "I was all set to get the police in and do a big story, and then I found out something that made me think again. It turned out that the girl's father was a cop — an inspector in the Marseille police department. You can imagine what a story that would have made.

"Well, I decided not to do it. I persuaded the girl to let me take her to a clinic run by a friend of mine, and then I went to see the father. His name's Andreis. He's a good man. We still have lunch a couple of times a year. I don't say we're close, but I have some credit there."

This was a side of her *louche* cousin that Sophie had never seen. "*Chapeau,* Philippe," she said. "Good for you. What happened to the girl?"

"It ended well. She married a doctor she met at the clinic, and I'm godfather to their little girl." Philippe stared at his empty glass with surprise, as though major evaporation had taken place while he wasn't looking.

Sam poured him some more wine. "Do you think he'd lend us one of his forensic guys for an hour or so?"

"I can ask. But he'll want to know the background, and I'll have to tell him."

Sam shrugged. "That's fine. We're not really going to be doing anything illegal. Tell him it's just a standard check, a routine procedure carried out by a conscientious and discreet insurance company that doesn't want to cause unnecessary annoyance or embarrassment. That's why we don't think it's worth bothering Reboul. Do you think he'll buy that? You can promise him that there'll be no theft, no breaking and entering." Sam paused to reconsider. "Well, no breaking and entering as long as we can get Vial out of the way for a couple of hours.

That's next on the list. Any ideas?" He raised his glass to Sophie and Philippe. "Here's to inspiration."

They parted company for the evening. Sophie wanted to check in with her office before having room service and an early night. Philippe thought he'd see if Inspector Andreis was at home. Sam, with somewhat mixed emotions, was going to call L.A. again and report on progress to Elena Morales. Their last conversation had ended on a distinctly low note. It was time, Sam felt, for some fences to be mended.

When he got through to Elena, he received a mono syllabic, frigid greeting. Now he knew what it felt like being a telemarketer on a bad day. He took a deep breath.

"Elena, I want you to hear me out. First of all, I don't want you to get the wrong idea about Sophie Costes. She's been a real help, and she's had a couple of great ideas." He might have been talking to Siberia, but at least she hadn't hung up. "Now, what you won't find on her C.V. is that she's planning to get married in the fall. He's called Arnaud — a nice, middle-aged guy from Bordeaux with an elderly mother and two Labradors named Lafite and Latour. Oh, and a château, apparently, but not a very big one."

"Is this what you called to tell me?"

Sam detected a hint of climate change coming down the line. "Partly, yes. I mean, I wanted to put the record straight. I didn't want you to think I was, well, you know . . ."

Elena let him dangle for a moment or two before replying. "OK, Sam. You've made your point." She sounded almost friendly. "So, how's it going down there?"

"Promising. I'll know for sure in a couple of days." Sam took Elena through what had happened since the first meeting with Reboul: the day with Vial, the discoveries in the cellar, the call to Lieutenant Bookman, and Philippe's efforts to help in resolving the question of the fingerprints. "In other words," said Sam as he came to the end of his report, "progress, but nothing definite. Nothing yet for Roth to get excited about."

At the mention of her client's name, Elena said something short and sharp in Spanish. It didn't sound complimentary.

"I'm sure you're right," said Sam. "You know, you should get away from him, take a few days off. Spoil yourself. They say Paris is pretty nice in the spring."

"Let me know about the prints. Oh, and Sam?" Her voice softened. "Thanks for the call."

She hung up. Diplomatic relations had been reestablished.

EIGHTEEN

Chez Félix, a spacious, well-kept bar on an unremarkable side street, is a brisk two-minute walk from Marseille police head-quarters on the Rue de l'Evêché. Thanks to this convenient location, and the added attraction that the bar's owner is a retired gendarme, Chez Félix has long been a favorite of police officers seeking liquid consolation after a hard day trading punches with the underworld. A popular feature of the bar is the section at the back, which has been divided into three small booths. Here, delicate matters can be discussed in private. It was in one of these booths that Philippe had arranged to meet Inspector Andreis.

The inspector, lean and grizzled, with the watchful eyes of a man who has seen more than his share of trouble, arrived just as Philippe was taking delivery of two glasses of pastis, a squat, potbellied jug of ice cubes and water, and a small saucer of green olives.

"I ordered for you," said Philippe as the two men shook hands. "You're still drinking Ricard?"

Andreis nodded and watched as Philippe added water to their glasses, turning the pale-yellow liquid cloudy. "That's enough," he said with a grin. "Don't drown it."

Philippe raised his glass. "Let's drink to retirement," he said. "How long is it now?"

"Another eight months, two weeks, and four days." Andreis looked at his watch. "Plus overtime. And then, thank God, I'm off to Corsica." He took a creased photograph from his pocket and placed it on the table. It showed a modest stone-built house set in a silvery-green sea of olive trees, planted in orderly lines that radiated out from the house like spokes in a wheel. "Three hundred and sixty-four trees. In a good year, that's about five hundred liters of oil." Andreis looked fondly at his future home. "I'll cultivate my olives, and I'll spoil my granddaughter. I'll eat those *figatelli* sausages and that *brocciu* cheese, and drink red wine from Patrimonio. I'll get a dog. I've always wanted a dog." He sat back in his chair, clasped his hands behind his head, stretched, and contemplated the rest of his life with a smile. "But somehow I don't think you wanted to see me just to hear about my old age." He cocked his head. Philippe started talking.

By the time the story had been told, the glasses were empty. The waiter came with more pastis and a fresh jug of iced water. Andreis nibbled on an olive and waited in silence until he had gone.

When he spoke, his voice was low and cautious. "I don't have to tell you what a powerful man Reboul is in this town. One doesn't want to get on the wrong side of him. Also, he's not a bad guy — a bit of a showman, it's true, but I've heard good things about him over the years." Andreis dabbed a finger in the tiny puddle of condensation that had formed around the base of his glass. "And, from what you say, we don't know for sure that he's done anything wrong." He raised a hand as Philippe leaned forward to speak. "I know, I know. Checking those prints is one way to find out. If it turns out that they match, well . . ."

"That would suggest a crime. Wouldn't it?"

"I suppose so. Yes, you're right." Andreis nodded and sighed. This was not something he wanted to get involved in. Poking your nose into the affairs of powerful and influential men had a way of ending badly for the owner of the nose. On the other hand, he didn't see how he could ignore it. It obviously had the makings of a big story. And the man sitting opposite him was a journalist; he wasn't going to let it go. Andreis sighed again, the virtuoso sigh of a man faced with a decision he'd rather not make.

"OK. I'll tell you what I can do. I can let you have a print man for a couple of hours, but only if you guarantee that Reboul and his people are kept out of it, at least until we've checked the prints. Can you promise that?"

"I think so. Yes."

"The last thing I need is Reboul calling his old friend the *préfet de police* to complain about the inappropriate use of official resources. So don't screw up." Andreis took a pen from his pocket, jotted down a name and number on a beer mat, and pushed it across to Philippe. "Grosso. We've worked together for twenty years. He's reliable, he's quick, and he's discreet. I'll have a word with him tonight. You can call him in the morning."

"It might work," said Sam. "If it were Reboul, I'm sure it would work. But with Vial? I don't know. Does he have a twinkle in his eye?"

Sophie took another piece of bread from the basket and used it to polish the last rich drops of *bourride* — Marseille's pungent fish soup — from her plate. They were having dinner in a fish restaurant by the port, and the topic of the evening was Florian Vial: how to get him out of the cellar while the bottles were being checked for prints.

Sophie's suggestion was simplicity itself: she would take him to lunch, a special lunch, to thank him for his help. Sam would be left in charge of the cellar, officially to catch up on the white wines he'd missed on the first visit; unofficially, to point out the suspected stolen bottles for the man who would be taking the prints.

It was true that the idea depended on Vial's being susceptible to a pretty woman, but here Sophie was optimistic. After all, Vial was French. And as she explained, Frenchmen of Vial's background and age had been brought up to appreciate the opposite sex, to enjoy their company, and to be gallant when dealing with them. She knew several men of a similar type in Bordeaux — charming, attentive, pleasantly flirtatious. They were gentlemen who liked women. Perhaps they would never go quite so far as to pinch a woman's bottom, but they'd certainly think about it. And they would never pass up the chance of a good lunch with an attractive companion.

There was an amused expression on Sophie's face as she looked over at Sam. He'd been wrestling with *calmars à l'encre,* tiny squid cooked in their ink, and judging by the dark stains on the napkin tucked into his shirt collar the squid had not surrendered without a fight.

"The problem is, Sam, that you don't understand French men. You'll see. It will be fine. Let me call Philippe to ask him if there's a good restaurant not far from the Palais." She took her napkin, moistened a corner of it with water from the ice bucket, and passed it over to him. "Here. You look as if you're wearing black lipstick." She left Sam to clean up and order coffee while she called her cousin.

The next morning, they arrived at the cellar a little after 10:30 to find Vial full of the joys of spring. A colleague in Beaune had just called to tell him that he had been selected to be the guest of honor at a dinner given by the Chevaliers du Tastevin. It was a considerable mark of respect, even more so because all the fine old traditions were going to be observed. The dinner — an intimate affair with invitations restricted to

211

two hundred prominent Burgundians —
would take place in the Clos de Vougeot,
the headquarters of the Chevaliers du
Tastevin. The Chevaliers would be wearing
their ceremonial long red robes for the oc-
casion. Music would be provided by the Joy-
eux Bourgignons, those masters of the
drinking song. And the wines, needless to
say, would be copious and exquisite.

Vial's high good humor was tempered
only slightly by the prospect of having to
give a speech, but Sophie reassured him.
"To hear you talk about wine," she said, "is
like hearing poetry. I could listen all day."
Before the flustered Vial could recover from
the compliment, Sophie went on. "But Florian — if I may — this has fallen very well.
I was going to ask you to lunch today, to
thank you for all your help. And now we
can celebrate at the same time. It's such
beautiful weather, I thought we might get a
table on the terrace at Péron. You will say
yes, won't you?" This time, Sam was certain
that she actually did flutter her eyelashes.

Vial made a point of consulting his diary,
but he was clearly delighted, and he put up
only token resistance and the merest sem-
blance of regret when Sophie told him that
Sam would have to stay behind to finish
the work he still had to do among the

white wines.

The next two hours passed slowly. Vial took Sophie off to introduce her to the glories of Reboul's red wines, with particular emphasis, this morning, on the Burgundies, where he could gain some inspiration for his forthcoming speech. Meanwhile, Sam found a distant corner among the champagnes where he could use his phone.

"Philippe? Sophie tells me that you've found a guy to take the prints. A plain-clothes guy, I hope."

Philippe chuckled. "Of course. You know what they say, my friend: if you want something done, ask a journalist. I spoke to him this morning. He says he's ready when we are."

"Well, today's the day. Lunchtime, around 12:45, and not before. Is that OK?"

"How do we get in?"

"The main gates are left open during the day, and you don't have to go anywhere near the house. Come to the delivery area in front of the cellar. It's marked, on the left of the drive. I'll let you in. And Philippe?"

"What?"

"Just make sure you don't turn up in a police car."

It would be difficult to imagine a more

agreeable place to have lunch on a fine sunny day than the terrace at Péron. High on the Corniche Kennedy, the restaurant offers an irresistible combination of fresh fish, fresh air, and a glittering view of the Frioul islands and the Château d'If. It is a setting to sharpen the appetite and bring on a holiday mood, and it had an instant effect on Florian Vial's sense of chivalry. Waving aside the waiter, he insisted on pulling out Sophie's chair and making sure she was comfortably settled before sitting down himself.

He rubbed his hands and took a deep breath of sea air. "Delightful, delightful. What an excellent choice, my dear madame. This is a real treat."

Sophie inclined her head. "Please call me Sophie. I thought perhaps we might start with a glass of champagne? But then you must choose the wine. I'm sure you have some little local favorites."

This set Vial off, as Sophie guessed it would, on a verbal tour of Provençal vineyards. "There have been vines here," he began, "since 600 B.C., when the Phocians founded Marseille." And from there, interrupted only by the arrival of champagne and menus, he took Sophie from Cassis to Bandol and beyond, going east to Palette and west to Bellet, with a lengthy detour to visit the underappreciated wines of the Langue-doc. The man was a walking encyclopedia, Sophie thought, and he had an enthusiasm for his subject that she found infectious and rather endearing.

They chose from the menu, and Vial selected a bone-dry white from Cassis to accompany the *loup de mer.* Sophie took advantage of the pause to ask Vial about himself, and his years with Reboul.

It was, as Vial said, a happy story with a tragic beginning. Thirty-five years ago, when Reboul was working on his early deals, he hired Vial's father as the financial director of what was then a fairly small company. The two men became friends. The company flourished. Young Florian, an only child, was showing signs of promise at university. The future looked rosy.

That future disappeared, in shocking fashion, one winter's night in Marseille. It was one of those rare years when freezing snow had fallen on the city. The roads were slick with black ice, conditions that very few Provençal drivers know how to handle. Vial's father and mother had been to the movies, and were driving home when a truck skidded sideways into their car, crush-ing it against a concrete wall. The car's occupants died instantly.

What happened then changed Vial's life. Reboul took his friend's son under his wing. He encouraged his early interest in wine and paid for him to attend a six-month course in viticulture at the wine institute of Carpentras, followed by a year's apprenticeship working for *négociants* in Burgundy and Bordeaux. During the year, it became apparent that the young man had an exceptional palate. This was confirmed by a final six months in Paris under the eye of the legendary Hervé Bouchon, who at the time was the best sommelier in France. Acting on Bouchon's recommendation, Reboul decided to take young Vial on as his corporate *caviste,* with a mandate to put together the best private cellar in France, and gave him a generous budget to help him do it.

"That was a long time ago," said Vial, "nearly thirty years. I don't know where I'd have been now if it hadn't been for him." His thoughtful expression brightened as the waiter came to take their orders for the last course. "If you permit, we might try with our dessert the closest thing Provence has to one of those Sauternes you Bordelais do so well. A glass of *muscat* from Beaumes-de-Venise. Can I tempt you?"

Vial's story had left Sophie feeling a little

confused, and she found herself beginning to hope that Reboul wasn't guilty. Even if he was, a small voice was telling her, it would be a shame if he didn't get away with it. She stole a glance at her watch and wondered how Sam was getting on.

Philippe and Grosso, a slight, neatly dressed man with a black attaché case that he described to Philippe as his box of tricks, had arrived in an unmarked car ten minutes before one o'clock, to find Sam waiting at the door. It was Philippe's first visit to the cellar, and the sight of row upon row of bottles stretching away beneath the vaulted ceilings of rose-pink brick rendered him almost speechless. *"Merde,"* was all he could say. *"Merde."* Grosso let out a soft whistle.

Sam led them over to the bin that contained the magnums of Pétrus. Grosso looked them over as he opened his attaché case and took out a halogen flashlight, a selection of brushes, a flat black box, and a small plastic canister. He sucked his teeth and flexed his fingers. *"On fait toutes les bouteilles?"* He looked at Sam. "All of the bottles?" Sam nodded. "And do you need DNA?" Another nod. Philippe was busy taking notes. He could see his scoop taking shape and, at this crucial stage of the story, the more detail he could pick up the better. He moved closer to Grosso to get a better view of what he was doing.

"Monsieur Grosso," he said, "I don't want to distract you, but I'm fascinated. Could you tell me a little about how you do this?"

Without looking up at Philippe, Grosso beckoned him closer. He had laid the first magnum on the ground and was shining his flashlight over it. "First, I do the visual examination," he said, "to check the surface for prints." He adjusted the angle of his flashlight. "Some of them can only be seen by the use of oblique light." He grunted, put the flashlight down, and unscrewed the lid of his canister, tilting it to one side so that Philippe could see the contents. "Metallic flake powder. The flakes are aluminum — they're the most sensitive, and they lift nicely." He took one of his brushes, and began to dab on the powder, sparingly, and with a light circular motion. "This is what we call a Zephyr brush; carbon fiber, with a mop head, which is less likely to disturb the print deposit." He finished with the brush and opened his black box, taking out some strips of clear adhesive tape. "Now I'm going to use this to lift the prints." Fingers moving with delicate precision, he applied tape to the scattered prints and then peeled off the strips before placing them on a sheet of clear acetate. "*Voilà.* You see? With this technique, there's no need to take photographs." The first magnum was replaced. Grosso moved on to the second.

Sam had been watching the ritual. It seemed to him agonizingly slow. He tapped Philippe on the shoulder and said, in a whisper, "Is there any way you can get him to speed things up?"

Philippe knelt on the floor next to Grosso to ask him. Sam couldn't hear what he said in response, but it sounded more like a growl than an answer, and Philippe was grinning as he looked up at Sam.

"He said, 'I can't dance faster than the music.' I think that means we should leave him alone to get on with it."

Sam told himself that Grosso's painstaking progress would seem even slower if he just stood there watching, and so he wandered off, down to the far end of the cellar. His eye was caught by a big pile of cartons neatly stacked in a corner and half-hidden behind Vial's golf cart. The cartons were marked with the ornate script he always thought of as vineyard copperplate: *Domaine Reboul, St. Helena, California.* He remembered Vial referring without any great enthusiasm to a property in the Napa Valley, and opened one of the cartons to see what kind of label he used for his American wine. But the carton was empty. So was the next one, and the one after that.

He called the hotel to see if he'd received a delivery from FedEx. Nothing yet. Doing his best to be patient, he retired to the impressive surroundings of the Rue de Corton-Charlemagne and turned over once again the questions that had been occupying a corner of his mind for the past few days: If the prints matched, what would he do? Confront Vial? Get the police officially involved? Pass the problem on to Elena and the people at Knox Insurance? All of the above? None of them?

The minutes passed; on leaden feet, but they passed. The next time he looked at his watch it was still not quite two o'clock. He went back to see how Grosso was getting on among the magnums. Only four to go.

Sophie had said she'd duck into the ladies' restroom and call when she and Vial were about to leave the restaurant.

Grosso continued; cool, calm, methodical.

"But this is quite delicious," said Sophie, after her first sip of Beaumes-de-Venise. "Halfway between sweet and dry. Lovely."

She raised an appreciative glass to Vial, who was nodding and smiling at her reaction. Not surprisingly, he had some comments to make about the wine's pedigree.

"The name of the grape, so the historians tell us, comes from the Italian *moscato.* That is to say, musk. Now, musk is very highly thought of among deer." Vial permitted himself a roguish twitch of the eyebrows. "It is the scent with which they — how shall I put it? — issue an invitation to deer of the opposite sex. Indeed, musk is also used as an ingredient in perfumes which, when worn by us humans, are supposed to have a similar effect." He picked up his glass, held it up to his nose, and took a long, considered sniff. "Delicate, very feminine — and yes, a hint of musk. Many sweet wines are fortified, but Beaumes-de-Venise is not. This gives it a gentler, more subtle taste than, for instance, the *muscat* of Frontignan." He took a sip and leaned back in his chair, his eyes going from Sophie to the view, and back to Sophie. With a shrug of reluctance, he looked at his watch.

"I can't tell you how much I've enjoyed our lunch," he said. "But I had no idea of the time. How it has flown by. I'm afraid we should be getting back."

"A quick coffee before we go," Sophie

said. "I'll order it on my way to the ladies' room."

Closing the door of the stall behind her, she checked the time as she waited for Sam to answer her call. Just past 2:15. "Has he finished?"

"Packing up now. Five minutes more, and they'll be out of here. Have a cognac or something."

"Five minutes, Sam. No longer."

In fact, dealing with the remains of the Beaumes-de-Venise, the coffee, and the bill took the best part of ten minutes, and by the time they arrived back at the cellar it was as they had left it, empty except for Sam. As they went through the door, they could hear him whistling "La Vie en rose."

NINETEEN

Sophie and Sam were setting off to walk back to their hotel. Behind them, the figure of Vial was framed in the cellar doorway. He waved as he watched them go down the drive and through the iron gates.

"How was lunch?" Sam asked.

"I think he enjoyed it." Sophie stopped to rummage in her handbag for her sunglasses. "Actually, I'm sure he did — I don't think I've ever been thanked so many times. But the whole thing made me uncomfortable. You know? He's a sweet man. And basically, lunch was a trap."

Sam watched two seagulls bickering in midair over the ownership of a scrap of fish. "Would you feel differently if Vial and Reboul were a couple of bastards?"

"Of course." She turned toward Sam and shrugged. "I know. It's not logical. A crime's a crime, no matter who committed it."

They walked on in a thoughtful silence.

When they reached the hotel, Sam went to the front desk. He came back to Sophie holding up a FedEx envelope. "The answer to all our questions," he said with a rueful grin. "Or maybe not."

Sam opened the envelope and took out the contents. Clipped to an official L.A.P.D. fingerprint sheet was a handwritten note in Bookman's hurried scrawl:

Sam —

Here are the prints. The guys who took them were disappointed that they didn't have to use force. Roth is not their favorite citizen.

A Dassault Falcon registered to the Groupe Reboul left Santa Barbara airport on December 27 for JFK. Ultimate destination Marseille. Flight plan details available if necessary.

Good luck.

P.S. I've taken a look at the French Laundry's wine list. Start saving up.

With a nod of the head, Sam passed the note to Sophie. "Congratulations — you've just been promoted to detective. It looks as though you could be right about the plane. It's only circumstantial evidence, but the timing's a perfect fit." He put the print sheet back in its envelope and reached for his phone. "We'd better get this to Philippe."

Grosso put down his magnifying glass and looked up from the sheet of Roth's prints he'd been studying. "Nice and clean," he said to Philippe. "There shouldn't be any problems. I'll let you know." He stood up and went toward the door of his office.

Philippe was having difficulty concealing his impatience or controlling his feet, which seemed to have lives of their own as they beat an urgent tattoo on the floor. "When do you think —"

Grosso cut him off with a wag of his finger. "This is not something one can do in a couple of minutes. You're looking for an unambiguous match, aren't you?"

Philippe nodded.

"Unambiguous," Grosso said again. "That means it has to be perfect. There can be no doubt, otherwise it won't stand up as evidence. I have to *know* it's a match, not just think it's a match. You understand? The process takes time." Grosso signaled the end of the meeting by opening the door. "I'll call you as soon as I'm sure, one way or another."

Philippe threaded his scooter through the tangle of traffic around the Vieux Port and headed up the hill toward the Sofitel, his mind racing. This was the final piece of the puzzle. If the prints matched, the story would almost write itself. To be sure, there would have to be some judicious editing, a little shading of the facts here and there. Sophie and Sam would probably not want their names mentioned, and there was the question of Inspector Andreis and his involvement. But, in well-worn journalistic style, any small omissions of this kind could always be justified by invoking the reporter's first commandment: thou shalt not reveal the names of thy sources (which even trumps that other hoary old favorite: the public has a right to know). Philippe felt a surge of optimism. It was all beginning to look very promising. He pulled up outside the hotel in an expansive mood, flourished a five-euro note, and told the startled doorman to park his scooter.

Looking for something to help them kill time, Sophie and Sam had decided to become tourists for the remainder of the afternoon and had taken a taxi up to Notre-Dame de la Garde, the basilica that dominates Marseille. Known locally as La Bonne Mère, and crowned by a thirty-foot-high statue of the Madonna and Child swathed in gold leaf, it is home to an astonishing collection of ex-votos. These have been donated over the centuries by sailors and fishermen who have narrowly escaped death at sea, and they come in many forms: marble plaques, mosaics, collages, scale models, paintings, life belts, flags, figurines — the interior walls of the church are smothered in them. Their common theme is gratitude, frequently expressed very simply. *"Merci, Bonne Mère"* is the message that one sees over and over again.

Sophie found these souvenirs of near misses fascinating, and often very touching; reminders of death, and celebrations of life. For Sam, whose experience of life at sea had been brief and bilious, they also brought back very vividly his profound dislike of boats. Not only were they cramped, damp, and uncomfortable; they lurched around in a capricious way, and they had a habit of sinking. After contemplating a particularly evocative painting of a three-master in high seas about to capsize, he went across to Sophie. "Isn't dry land wonderful?" he murmured. "I'll wait for you outside. I'm worried that if I stay here much longer I'll get seasick."

He had spent an hour in the semi-gloom of the church, and it took his eyes a few moments to adjust to the glare of the early-evening sun, and a few moments more to take in the view. Even though his time in Marseille had been amply decorated with postcard views — from various points in the hotel or from Reboul's living room in the Palais du Pharo — what he saw from the esplanade in front of La Bonne Mère was quite breathtaking: looking north, the Vieux Port, and the old *quartier* of Le Panier; looking west, the stylish nineteenth-century villas of Le Roucas Blanc, and the beaches of the Prado; and to the south, a ripple of tiled rooftops leading to the shimmering sweep of the sea. He was wondering if Reboul ever came up here to compare this view with what he had at home, when his phone rang.

"Sam? Where are you?" Philippe's voice was low and urgent, almost a whisper.

"On top of the world. The big church with the view."

"Well, get back to the hotel. We need to talk."

"What's happened?"

"Grosso just called. On three of the magnums, the prints correspond to Roth's. He says there's no doubt about it: an unambiguous match."

Sam wasn't sure whether he was pleased

or disappointed, and during the taxi ride it became clear that Sophie, too, had very mixed feelings. But when they got back to the hotel, it was to find a man untroubled by doubts or misgivings. Philippe had settled himself at a corner table with three *flûtes* and a loaded ice bucket. The glint of gold foil on the neck of the bottle was a sure sign of champagne.

Philippe got to his feet with a smile almost as wide as his open arms. "So, *mes chers,* we have solved the case, no? We have proof." He bent down to administer to the champagne, filling the *flûtes* with exaggerated care before passing them around. Raising his own glass and inclining his head toward the others, he said, "Congratulations to us all. This is going to be some surprise for Reboul, eh? Oh, I forgot to tell you — I have a good contact at the airport. Perhaps he can find out for us what was brought in by Reboul's plane from California last December. You know, it's funny. One thing leads to another, and then — *pouf!* — all kinds of secrets come out."

Sam took a reflective sip of his champagne. "There's something that bothers me about this whole business," he said, "and that's motive. If ever there was a man who has everything, it's Reboul. Success, money, all the trappings. Hot-and-cold-running girlfriends, a private palace, a private jet, a yacht — and, God knows, more than enough wine to last him the rest of his life." He paused, and looked at Philippe. "Why did he do it? Why take the risk?"

"But, Sam," said Philippe, shaking his head, "you don't understand the French."

It was a gap in Sam's education that had already been pointed out to him several times over the past few days. "Right. Sophie already told me. So?"

Philippe continued. "Don't forget that Chauvin was a Frenchman. We *invented* chauvinism. Some might even mistake this for arrogance." At this, Philippe paused to flex his eyebrows, as though astonished that anyone could think such a thing of his countrymen. "We are passionate about our country, our culture, our cooking, our *patrimoine.* And nobody is more passionate than our friend Reboul. He even pays French taxes, for God's sake. You've read the articles in the dossier. He's always sounding off about the horrors of globalization, the erosion of French values, the tragedy of French assets falling into foreign hands — businesses, property, and, *bien sûr,* our best wines. To read about all that *premier cru* Bordeaux sitting in a cellar in Hollywood

— Hollywood, of all places! — would be an affront, an outrage, a bone in his throat. And then, of course, we must not forget another factor, a most important factor: the sporting challenge. *Mais oui.*" Philippe nodded to himself as he took a sip of champagne.

Sophie and Sam looked puzzled. "Well," said Sam, "I'm not sure if I buy the idea of robbery for purely patriotic reasons, but let's say you're right. Where does sport come into it? Is this something else about the Frenchman that I don't understand?"

Philippe settled back in his chair, very much the professor bringing enlightenment to a promising student. "No, not this time. It's more to do with being rich than being French. It's the feeling a man develops, after many years of wealth and power, that he can have anything he wants and do anything he wants. *Folie des grandeurs.* He can indulge his little fancies. He can take chances. After all, if anything goes wrong, he can be sure that his money will protect him." Philippe's eyes went from Sophie to Sam, trying to assess their reactions. "That, I think you will agree, is true in general. Now we come to the particular. Now we come to Reboul."

A group of young businessmen — with

231

dark suits, short haircuts, and oversized watches — arrived at the next table. Philippe lowered his voice, so that Sophie and Sam had to lean forward to hear him.

"Reboul set up his empire very efficiently. The businesses are run by men he has worked with for a long time. He trusts them, and pays them well. In return, they deliver profits; year in, year out. The Groupe Reboul runs *sur les roulettes,* like clockwork — it's well known for that. As for Reboul himself, what does he do with his time? He attends a few board meetings, just to keep an eye on things; he cultivates contacts; he gives interviews; he hosts a few high-level dinners. He has his soccer team and his yacht to play with. But where is the challenge? He's done it all. He's won. He's bored. I'm convinced of it."

Sam was nodding. He had met a few billionaires in California with the same problem. Some, the fortunate ones, were able to distract themselves with elaborate projects like the Americas Cup; others went from one corporate acquisition to the next, from one wife to the next, highly competitive, often surprisingly insecure, and occasionally extremely weird. Reboul didn't appear to suffer from insecurity or weirdness. But boredom? Sam could easily imagine a man like him getting bored.

Philippe's voice dropped even lower. "And so we have a man with unlimited amounts of money, a man with time on his hands, a man who is devoted, as he is always telling us, to France and everything that is French. What could be more amusing than to play this little game, to plan and execute the perfect robbery that would bring a national treasure back to the land it came from? And then perhaps have his friend the chief of police to a dinner washed down with stolen wine. There is the sport. There is the challenge. *Voilà.*" Philippe rubbed his hands together and reached for the champagne.

Sam had to admit that he'd known of crimes committed for similarly whimsical reasons. Indeed, he had committed one or two of them himself, a thought that lodged in his mind, waiting to be considered later. "Sophie?" he said. "What do you think?"

Sophie was frowning as she looked at her cousin. "I think Philippe has written his article already. But yes, what he says is possible." She studied the tiny pinpoints of bubbles rising from the bottom of her glass, and shrugged. "So, my two detectives, what do we do about it?"

"Let's sleep on it," said Sam. "But first,

I'd better call L.A. and bring them up to speed."

There was a steely, hostile edge to Elena's voice when she picked up Sam's call. He had heard that tone in her voice before, when things between them had been going wrong, and it always made him want to duck. She was formidable when roused.

"Elena, don't bite," he said. "It's me. Your man in the field."

Sam could hear her take a deep breath and let it out slowly. "Sam, I'm sorry. But I've just had the daily earful from Danny Roth. I thought it was him calling back. He's always doing that. I think he knows it drives me crazy." Elena followed this with a short but blistering tirade in Spanish, ending with a fusillade of expletives and another deep breath. "I needed that. OK, now tell me what's happening."

"The good news is that I'm pretty sure We've found the wine. Roth's fingerprints are on some of the bottles in Reboul's cellar, and the guy who did the match works for the police down here. So it's solid evidence."

"That's wonderful, Sam. Great work. Congratulations." But she didn't sound ready to celebrate just yet. "Tell me I'm

234

wrong, but I get the feeling there's some bad news as well."

"Could be. Reboul may have done it, but he's smart. It's more than likely he's covered his tracks with fake invoices and all kinds of paperwork. If that's what we find he's done, we can say hello to the lawyers, and I don't have to tell you what that means: a million bucks in legal fees, and the case tied up for months. Maybe years."

"Not to mention a lawsuit to decide who pays the legal fees."

"Exactly. The problem is we won't know how he's covered himself until we make a move on him, and then there's no going back. So I'm beginning to have a few thoughts about plan B."

"Does it involve homicide and a well-known L.A. entertainment lawyer? Can I come?"

"You know me, Elena. I don't do homicides. Listen, there's something I need to know. In a case like this, what's the bottom line? What do you absolutely have to have in order to avoid paying out that claim?"

"OK. It boils down to three things: discovery, identification, and condition. We have to know the whereabouts of the stolen goods. We need cast-iron confirmation that they *are* the stolen goods. And we have to be satisfied that they are still in good condition; ideally, the same condition they were in when stolen. There are dozens of supplementary details, but essentially if those three points stack up, then we're off the hook."

"And who does all the checking? Is it you or is it Roth?"

"Are you kidding? Would you take Roth's word for anything? You know that old saying, 'Good morning, he lied'? Well, that's Danny Roth. No, the verification is done by us — in this case, by me and a couple of experts — and then we get Roth to sign off on it. And then I push him over a cliff."

"Thank you, Ms. Morales. That will be all. I'll be in touch."

"What's plan B?"

"Trust me. You don't want to know about it. Good night, Elena."

"Good night, Sam."

TWENTY

The night was dragging, as if the clocks had slowed down, and Sam's mind was far too busy to let him sleep. Scotch, normally a sure soporific, had no effect. Even a CNN special on the renaissance of the Nigerian banking system was unable to work its soothing magic. He was wide, wide awake.

He put on a sweater and went out onto his terrace, hoping the sharp night air would succeed where whisky and television had failed. He stared at the moon hanging above the Vieux Port. Almost full. He checked his watch. Almost three a.m. He wondered where he'd be this time tomorrow. He wondered if it would work, if he'd thought of everything. And he wondered if the others would go along with it.

Dawn found him still on the terrace; cold and stiff, but not at all tired. In fact, he felt as though his sleepless night had given him a shot of adrenaline, and he was impatient to get on with the day. He called room service to order breakfast, and stood under a scalding shower until his skin started to redden through its California tan.

He did his best to dawdle over coffee and the *Herald Tribune,* but it was still too early to call Sophie and Philippe. He decided to take a walk, and on leaving the hotel instinctively turned right, in the direction of the Palais du Pharo.

The great iron gates hadn't yet been opened for the day, and he stood looking through the black bars toward the immense green carpet of lawn that led up to the house. Vial wouldn't be in his cellar much before ten, and the domestic staff who worked for Reboul would be taking advantage of his absence in Corsica to have an extra half hour in bed. It was surprisingly quiet for a spot so close to the center of the city. Behind him, he could hear the murmur of traffic as Marseille hurried about its early-morning business, and the mournful hoot of a ship's siren coming from the direction of the docks beyond the Vieux Port. The sound prompted him to set off down the hill to the Quai des Belges, to see the catch of the day being set out for the fish market.

The fishing boats normally get in between

8:00 and 8:30 a.m., but the ladies of the market are there before them, their stands empty and waiting and freshly scrubbed. A traditional feature of the market — almost a tourist attraction in itself — is the often ripe vocabulary of these ladies, delivered with relish by voices powerful enough to compete with a force-eight mistral. Sam regretted that his level of French wasn't quite high enough, or perhaps low enough, and most of the unprintable nuances escaped him. He thought he'd like to come back with Philippe as his interpreter.

The boats had started to tie up to the quay, and the badinage of the ladies increased in volume, accompanied by the soft slap of fish being arranged on the stands, eyes still bright and scales gleaming. In ones and twos, the first customers started to arrive. In the time-honored manner of the French when shopping for anything edible, they looked deeply suspicious as they went from one stand to the next — peering into the eyes of a *rascasse,* sniffing the gills of a *galinette,* weighing the attractions of a grilled *daurade* against the delights of a *bouillabaisse.*

Sam's first and only encounter with this legendary dish — an experience that still made him shudder — had been in New

Orleans, when he had been persuaded to try something called *bouillabaisse Créole.* It had been sufficiently nasty to make him ask the waiter about the ingredients. These turned out to include flour, oysters, margarine, and chicken broth. It was an odd mixture for a fish stew. He promised himself a genuine *bouillabaisse* one day. It was another reason to return to Marseille, a city he found himself liking more and more.

Without realizing, he had drifted close enough to one of the stands to arouse the sales instinct of the proprietor, a vast, weather-beaten woman wearing a faded baseball cap and heavy-duty rubber gloves. *"Eh, monsieur!"* she bellowed at him. *"Comme il est beau, ce loup!"* She picked up a large and splendid sea bass and thrust it toward him, a smile splitting her brick-red face. Sam made the mistake of nodding and smiling back. Before he could stop her, she had picked up a knife and gutted the *loup* with lethal speed and precision before starting to wrap it. Not a woman to argue with, Sam thought. He bought the fish.

As he started off back to the hotel, the clammy package tucked under his arm, he made a mental note to write down the recipe the woman had passed on to him. So simple, she had said, even a man like him could do it. Make two deep cuts in your fish, one on each side, and stick two or three short pieces of fennel in each cut. Paint the fish with olive oil. Grill on each side for six or seven minutes. Using a fireproof serving dish, place the fish on a bed of dried fennel stalks. Warm a soup ladle filled with Armagnac, set light to it, and pour it over the serving dish. The fennel catches fire, scents the air, and flavors the fish. *"Une merveille,"* she had said.

His phone was ringing as he came into the hotel lobby.

"Where are you?" said Philippe. "Ah, there you are — I see you." He waved at Sam from the table where he was sitting with coffee and newspapers.

"I'll be right back," said Sam. "I have to get rid of this fish."

Philippe showed no surprise. "Of course," he said, as though a man wearing a business suit and a large dead fish were an everyday sight. "Sophie's on her way down."

Sam approached the desk of the concierge, holding his catch in front of him with both hands. "My compliments to the chef," he said, placing the fish on the desk, "and I would like him to have this *loup de mer.* It's fresh from the market."

The concierge inclined his head and

smiled. "Of course, monsieur. How very kind. I'll see that he gets it immediately. Will there be anything else?"

Sam went back to join the others, with a mental tip of the hat to the concierge for his *sangfroid*. Jeeves would have been proud of him.

There was an air of expectancy about Sophie and Philippe, and Sam wasted no time getting started. "I have an idea," he said. "But before I get to that, let me go over some of the background again. Stop me if you disagree with any of it. Now, we're sure beyond a reasonable doubt that the stolen wine is in the cellar, and we have Roth's fingerprints as proof. So we could blow the whistle on Reboul and go home. But what would happen then? The police would be all over him and Vial, and lawyers would get involved. If Reboul has covered his tracks — and I'm pretty sure he will have done that very thoroughly — all we can be sure of is that this whole business will take months to resolve. Probably years. Meanwhile, the wine will be taken into custody as evidence. And there will probably be a press embargo that would stop Philippe writing about a delicate case affecting a prominent man's reputation. Reboul's lawyers would make sure of that. I'd bet on it." Sam stopped to let this sink in. "Any questions so far?"

Sophie said nothing. Philippe chewed his lower lip and looked thoughtful. Sam went on. "There's another aspect to this which I don't think any of us anticipated. It turns out that Reboul and Vial seem to be pretty good guys. We like them, and we wouldn't want to see them in trouble, and possibly in jail. Am I right, Sophie?"

Sophie nodded. "I think it would be a shame."

"Me, too." Sam rubbed his eyes. They were beginning to feel gritty from his lack of sleep. "OK. Now, I spent most of last night on this, and I think it could work. Worth a try, anyway, because it has a lot going for it." Sam counted off the points on his fingers. "Number one, it lets Reboul and Vial off the hook. Number two, it gives Philippe another, maybe better story — a mystery, and he would be in the middle of it. Number three, it means that Sophie and I will have done our job for the people at Knox Insurance. We'll have tracked down the wine. There's only one snag. Up till now, we haven't committed any serious crime — perhaps a little harmless misrepresentation, that's all. But what I have in mind is illegal."

Philippe was back in his preferred position, perched on the edge of his seat, his feet starting to twitch. "How illegal?"

"I thought I'd steal the wine."

Sophie laughed, and shook her head. "*Mais c'est fou.* You're crazy."

Philippe held up his hand. "Just a minute." He looked behind him as he leaned forward, every inch the conspirator. Anyone watching would have marked him down instantly as a man discussing a guilty secret. His voice was little more than a whisper. "You've worked out how to do it?"

"Absolutely."

Sophie had stopped laughing. "But Sam, we would be the obvious suspects. Reboul tells the police about this strange couple spending days in his cellar, and they find us, and then it is not him in jail. It's us. No?"

Sam shook his head. "We could argue that what we're doing here is to recover stolen property on behalf of the client of an international, highly reputable insurance company. Our methods are a bit unorthodox, that's all. But more important: what's Reboul going to say? Someone's stolen the wine I stole? I don't think so. No matter how good his lawyers are, he won't want Interpol on his back. No, I'm pretty sure he'll keep quiet."

Philippe gave up chewing his lip to pour some more coffee. "Sam, you said something about a better story." He looked at Sophie, and added quickly, "That is, if we decide to go ahead."

"Right. It begins with that old favorite, the anonymous tip-off — you must have had dozens of them before. Sometimes the motive is revenge, sometimes it's guilt, sometimes it's just mischief. Anyway, you receive a call from a stranger. He refuses to identify himself. He tells you about an extraordinary cache of wine that has been left in a remote spot — We'll come to that later — and he tells you that it has been stolen. Perhaps he's stolen it himself and can't unload it. But he doesn't go into details. In fact, there are no other details. Just directions that lead to the hiding place. You don't really believe him, but you go there. What a surprise: you find the wine, just as your anonymous caller said. And there's chapter one of your story."

Philippe nodded slowly. "Not a bad start. And I think I can see where it's going."

"I'm sure you can. You investigate. You call all your contacts. And little by little, maybe article by article, you pick up clues that lead you to Los Angeles, where you interview Danny Roth and get his take on how the wine was stolen: Christmas Eve, the crooked caretaker, the ambulance, everything. That part is clear. The other part — who stole the wine — remains an unsolved mystery; Reboul and Vial are left out of it." Sam looked from Sophie to Philippe. "What do you think?"

"I like it," said Philippe. "It could make a great series, like a *feuilleton* on television." His feet danced a little jig of approval.

They both turned to look at Sophie.

It took some time to convince her that larceny was their best option. She tried to argue that they could just forget the whole thing and go home, but Sam reminded her it was too late for that: he had told Elena Morales. Knox International already knew the wine had been found, and they would follow up, with or without Sam. And so, after considerable soul-searching on Sophie's part, it was agreed. They would steal the wine.

Philippe was able to provide the solution to the next problem, which was where the wine could be hidden. His grandmother had owned a farm and a few acres of land on the Claparèdes, an isolated area in the Luberon. When Philippe was growing up, he used to spend the summers there, a pleasant family tradition that ended when his grandmother died. Unfortunately, she had left no will, which provoked a bitter inheritance squabble — not uncommon in France — between relatives who thought they were entitled to the property. This had been going on for thirteen years so far, and showed no sign of resolution. Meanwhile, the farm was uninhabited and sadly neglected. None of the competing relatives was prepared to pay to maintain a property that might eventually go to someone else — an undeserving wretch of a cousin, for instance, or the universally detested Aunt Hortense. Apart from its extremely remote location, Philippe said, the property had the advantage of a good-sized cellar, where the wine could be kept without risk of deterioration.

"Sounds ideal," said Sam. "Can you get in?"

"The key's hidden under a stone behind the well. Or there's a shutter that never worked on the kitchen window. One way or another, getting in won't be a problem."

"Fine. The next thing is transportation, and I don't think your scooter's going to be enough. Are you OK to drive a small van?"

Philippe sat up straight, an indignant expression on his face. "All Frenchmen can drive anything."

"I thought so. We'll rent something this afternoon." Sam turned to Sophie. "Here's

247

where I'm going to need your help. I have to get into the house before it's shut up for the night. My excuse for wandering around is that we have to take reference photographs, and the best time for that is in the evening, when the light's really good. As soon as I get the chance, I'll disappear. If Vial or anyone else asks where I am, you can say I had to go into town for a meeting. You keep taking photographs until the staff begins to leave, then get back to the hotel."

Sophie was frowning. "Then what happens?"

"Let's get something to eat. I'll tell you over lunch."

At the mention of lunch, Philippe stood up and rubbed his hands. "Just one question," he said. "When do we do this?"

Sam looked at his watch. "In about six hours."

TWENTY-ONE

The hours after lunch were spent finalizing the evening's plans. Philippe rented an unmarked white van — he described it as a plumber's Ferrari — easily big enough to hold fifty cases of wine. Sophie called Vial to tell him that she and Sam would be taking exterior reference shots in the gardens around the house for an hour or so in the evening, and suggested that they meet for a drink afterward. Vial didn't need to be asked twice.

Sam spent the afternoon in a state of enforced inactivity, a kind of expectant limbo. There was little he could do now but hope for the best; luck had to be with him during the first crucial stage. He took his second shower of the day and changed into an outfit suitable for nocturnal burglary: dark-blue trousers, dark-blue T-shirt, dark-blue windbreaker. Everything else he threw into his suitcase. He checked and rechecked the batteries in his camera and penlight, and charged his phone. He went once again through the list of stolen wines before putting it in his pocket. He paced up and down his terrace, for once oblivious to the view. He came close to twiddling his thumbs. He was more than ready to go.

The sun was beginning its daily dip toward the horizon, and the slanting golden light was a photographer's dream as Sophie and Sam made their way up the entrance steps to the Palais du Pharo. Before they had a chance to ring the bell, the front door opened. The housekeeper, an elegant, gray-haired woman in a crisp linen dress, came out to greet them.

"Florian told me to expect you," she said. "You must let me know if there's anything I can do to help."

Sophie thanked her. "We'll be outside for most of the time," she said. "It's such a marvelous light between now and sunset. But perhaps we could come indoors for one final shot through the living room window — you know, that moment just before the sun disappears into the sea. We saw it when we were with Monsieur Reboul, and it was quite spectacular."

The housekeeper nodded. "I'll leave the terrace door open for you. I'm sorry you won't have a chance to see Monsieur Reboul tonight. But he gets back tomorrow, and I'm sure he'd love to see the pictures." With a smile and a regal flutter of her hand, she turned and went back inside.

"What a bit of luck," said Sam as they walked around the house toward the gardens overlooking the sea. "Tomorrow would have been too late. I imagine there's always a reception committee when Reboul gets back from one of his trips." He took his camera from his pocket and turned it on. "She's quite a grand lady for a housekeeper, isn't she?"

Sophie looked up at the towering façade: three floors and countless windows. Reboul could have lodged a small army in there. "It's quite a grand house." She stopped, and put a hand on Sam's arm. He could feel it was trembling. "Sam, I'm nervous."

He squeezed her hand and grinned. "Me too. That's the way it should be. It's when you're not nervous that you get careless. Listen — you've been great all through this, and it's nearly over. One last effort and you're done." He took her arm and guided her through the garden, his free hand panning the camera across the view. "Now, you're in charge. Tell me where to start, and remember to point at what you want me to

251

shoot. Wave your arms about. Stamp your foot. Tear your hair out. Make like a creative director. You'll have an audience. I'm pretty sure our friend indoors will be keeping her eye on us to make sure we're not disturbing the lavender."

They photographed the terrace, the clipped formality of the gardens, the 180-degree view, all the time conscious of the sun's slow progress as it dropped closer and closer to the sea. Just before they had finished, Sam stopped, put his phone to his ear, and went through the motions of taking a call before putting the phone back in his pocket. "My excuse for leaving," he said, and passed the camera over to Sophie. "Let's go inside for the shot through the window. This is where I disappear. Can you take pictures with your fingers crossed?"

They went into the house from the terrace, and crossed a small lobby before reaching the living room door. It was open. They were well inside the room before they realized they were not alone.

"I'm sure you have made some lovely photographs. It's such a perfect evening." The housekeeper got up from the ornate little desk in front of the window where she'd been making notes and came toward them, gracious and smiling, the last person

Sam wanted to see.

He pasted an answering smile onto his face. "I'm so glad we caught you," he said. "I've just had a call reminding me that I'm late for a meeting in Marseille, but I wanted to thank you before I left. Sophie's taking over for the last couple of shots."

The housekeeper put on a diplomatic expression that managed to convey both disappointment and understanding. "What a pity you have to rush." She made a move toward the door. "You must let me show you —"

Sam held up a hand. "No, no, no. Please don't bother. I'll see myself out. Thanks again." And with that, he hurried from the room, closing the door behind him.

He crossed the main entrance lobby and slipped into the dining room. Tiptoeing past the twenty-seat table with its high-backed tapestry chairs, he came to the serving alcove and the heavy swing door that led to the kitchen. He put his ear to the crack between door and wall: nothing but the muted hum of refrigerators. He went through, past the gleaming array of stainless steel and copper, and into the back kitchen. In front of him was the door to the stairs that led down to the cellar; locked, as he had expected. He checked his watch. Six-fifteen. Sophie was meeting Vial at 6:30, and taking him back to the hotel bar.

Sam braced himself for an uncomfortable quarter of an hour and opened the door of the dumbwaiter. What had Vial called it? "The elevator for bottles. There is no turbulence. The wine arrives relaxed." He hoped he could do the same.

In fact, the elevator for bottles was little more than a long box, hand-operated by the old-fashioned combination of rope and pulley. But it was a substantial piece of work, solid enough to hold the weight of half a dozen cases of wine and tall enough for the cases to fit one on top of another in a single stack. Almost coffin-shaped. Sam tried not to dwell on that as he caught hold of the thick rope that operated the pulley and wedged himself gingerly into the narrow space, wincing at the sound of the pulley creaking under his weight. He closed the door and drew a deep breath. The darkness around him held the faintly musty smell of corks and stale wine, the souvenir of a bottle that had leaked during its journey upstairs. He fed the pulley rope through his hands, lowering himself slowly and with infinite care until he felt the soft thump that told him he'd arrived at cellar level.

Florian Vial put the finishing touches to

the jaunty upward sweep of his moustache and walked down the cellar to the stairway leading into the house, passing within six feet of the crouching figure inside the dumbwaiter. He was looking forward to seeing Sophie again, all the more after receiving her call to say that Sam wouldn't be able to join them. A pleasant enough young man, of course, but Vial much preferred the intimacy of a *tête-à-tête* with Sophie, and there was the added advantage that they could speak French, a language made for gallantries.

Sam heard Vial's footsteps on the flagstones of the cellar floor, and gave him another few minutes to get up the stairs and into the house. He was by now beginning to suffer from mild claustrophobia and the onset of a cramp. His thigh muscles felt as though they had been stretched to the snapping point, and he was sure he'd picked up a splinter in his backside. But he'd made it. The cellar was his for the night, and the hours of physical labor ahead of him would come as a relief after his ordeal in the dumbwaiter.

The pulley rope gave a final creak as he hauled himself out, and he stood for a few moments in the darkness, stretching the kinks out of his body. Even though the risk of being detected was minimal, he had decided to wait for a couple of hours before turning on the cellar lights and starting work. By then, just about everyone in Marseille would be observing the sacred ritual of dinner.

Guided by the thin beam of his flashlight, he made his way down to the far end of the cellar, where he found everything as he had remembered it. The golf cart was parked in its place by the door, and the empty cartons from Domaine Reboul were piled up in the corner. These would have to be replaced with unmarked cartons, but there would be plenty of time later for that. He went into Vial's office, settled himself in Vial's chair, and put his feet up on Vial's desk. Philippe answered his call after the first ring.

"So far, so good," said Sam.

"You're in the cellar?"

"I'm in the cellar. I'll be starting to pack up the wine in a couple of hours. Let's just go through the drill again."

"*Bon.* When all the wine is packed, you will call me. The van's parked by the Vieux Port. At that time of night, it will take me three minutes to reach the Palais."

"Good. Now, I'll make sure the gates are open. Remember to switch off your lights just before you turn into the drive. I don't want anyone in the house to see any head-lights. Take the left fork off the main drive. I'll blink my flashlight to guide you into the delivery area. The cases will be stacked up outside the cellar. Loading them into the van will take five minutes, tops. Then We'll be out of here."

"Roger that."

"Roger what?"

"It's army talk. I heard it on a TV show."

Sam rolled his eyes in the darkness. He'd forgotten Philippe's fondness for all things military. "Oh, one other thing. How long will it take to get where we're going?"

"The van isn't built for speed, but We'll be on the *autoroute* for a lot of the way. I think an hour and a half, not much more."

"OK. We're all set. See you later."

Sam's confidence was increasing now that he was getting close to the finish. Something could go wrong, of course; something always could. But he allowed himself a few moments of optimism as he considered facts and possibilities.

The most encouraging of these was his almost total isolation from the outside world. There were no windows in the cellar, so there would be no chinks of light to give him away. There was no chance of anyone hearing him, thanks to the soundproofing provided by massive walls, massive ceilings, and, above them, several feet of earth. And best of all, the alarm system, which he'd checked during previous visits, was activated only by someone trying to break in, not by someone letting himself out. That made two cellars — this one and Roth's — where electronic protection wasn't all it should be. He made a mental note to tell Elena. She'd welcome any excuse to read the riot act yet again to Roth about his sloppy security arrangements.

Elena occupied his thoughts pleasantly as he sat in the darkness, and he started to think ahead, beyond the night's work. How would she react to criminal methods being used to solve a crime? Personally, she might turn a blind eye. Professionally, she'd have a few problems, and she wouldn't hesitate to give him a hard time. But not for long. In the insurance business, as in most other enterprises involving large amounts of money, the end tends to justify the means. A healthy bottom line excuses most sins. It's a wicked old world, he reflected, as he leaned back in Vial's chair and waited for the hours to go by.

He must have dozed. When he next looked at his watch it was just before ten; time to go to work. He stood up, rubbed his eyes, and found the switch by the main door. The cellar looked bigger and more mysterious at night than it had during the day, when sunshine had flooded in through the open doors. Now the vaulted ceilings were thick with shadow, and the pools of light cast by the hanging lamps seemed to stretch away forever.

Sam loaded a batch of empty cartons into the golf cart and set off, the tires thrumming on the flagstone pathway that separated the reds from the whites. His first stop was the Rue des Merveilles, that distinguished address where Château Lafite rubbed aristocratic shoulders with Château Latour. He took the list of Roth's wines from his pocket and smoothed it out on the passenger seat:

'61 Latour, 98 bottles. He went along the rows of bins, looking at the slate tickets marked in chalk that identified the vintage years until he came to 1961. There must have been at least three hundred bottles, he calculated, as he started to fill the empty cartons, and there was no means of knowing if the ninety-eight bottles he took were actually Roth's. But, as he told himself, Roth wasn't going to complain. He settled into a rhythm: take two bottles from the bin, check the vintage on each label to make

sure, slide the bottles into their individual compartments in the carton, straighten up, go back to the bin. As each carton was filled it was placed on the flatbed behind the seats of the golf cart.

He paused to look at his watch. It had taken more than thirty minutes to pack fewer than a hundred bottles of Latour. At this rate, he had about three hours to go, plus the trips back and forth in the golf cart. That would see him finished sometime between two and three a.m. He wondered how Philippe was managing to contain his impatience.

'53 Lafite, 76 bottles. As he bent and straightened and shuttled between the bins and the golf cart, some of the comments of Florian Vial came back to him. When describing the Lafite, his extravagant compliments had been partially muffled by the frequent kisses he applied to his fingertips. Even so, some gems that Vial had taken from his fellow wine experts' overblown descriptions had come through loud and clear. Sam remembered one purple patch in particular that had started off quietly enough with "firm yet supple, soft and yet assertive," going on to "finesse, fragrance, and depth of flavor" mixed with "elegance, authority, and breeding that unfolded splen-

260

didly in the mouth," and ending with this rousing climax: "so grand and sublime as to afford a symposium of all other wines." All of this Vial had quoted, in English, from memory. At the other end of the prose scale had been his own more down-to-earth opinion that "in the end, the best wine is the wine you like."

'82 Figeac, 110 bottles. Sam tried to picture the château in his mind while he checked and packed the bottles: stone columns, an allée of fine old trees, a gravel drive. Sophie had told him that the present owner's grandfather had treated Figeac as a holiday home, coming down from Paris only rarely, and leaving the château closed for the rest of the year. Sam found that hard to imagine. He shook his head at the thought and started work on another empty carton. It occurred to him that it was not unlike packing bullion. How much in dollar value had he shifted so far? A million? Two?

'70 Pétrus, 48 bottles, 5 magnums. As featured in the *L.A. Times,* Sam thought, putting the first of the magnums into its nest of cardboard. Was this the one that Danny Roth had been cradling in the photograph? Who had shown the article to Reboul? Who had planned and done the job? Whoever they were, Sam couldn't fault

them professionally. Even Bookman had said that it was as close to a perfect heist as he'd seen. A shame, really, that there was no chance of sitting down with Reboul one day over a drink and filling in some of the gaps.

'83 Margaux, 140 bottles. Another question: who had Roth used to buy for him? Someone who knew his stuff, that was sure. There wasn't a single doubtful bottle in the collection. It was all wine of the very highest quality. When doing his research before leaving L.A., Sam had been amazed at the rise in value of the 1980s vintages of *premier cru* Bordeaux. Between 2001and 2006, for example, Margaux had gone up by 58 percent, and Lafite by 123 percent. It was no wonder Roth was climbing the walls. God knows what it would cost him now to refill his cellar.

The cartons were becoming heavier and heavier, the trips in the golf cart offering only brief moments of relief for an aching back. Sam longed for a massage and a drink.

'75 Yquem, 36 bottles. The last three cartons, and a wine that brought out the best (or worst) in wine writers, those whose mission in life is to describe the indescribable. "Fat, rich, and luscious," or "huge and voluptuous" — Sam had seen the phrases

time and time again, and they never failed to conjure up images not of a glass of wine but of the kind of statuesque woman Rubens liked to paint. With a feeling of huge and voluptuous satisfaction, he loaded the final carton onto the golf cart and drove down to the other cartons piled up by the cellar door.

He was nearly there. He turned off the lights and eased open the door. The night smelled cool and clean after the humid cellar air, and he sucked in a deep, welcome breath as he looked down the drive. He could make out the form of the gates silhouetted against the lights of the boulevard. A car passed, going up the hill, and then silence. Marseille, it seemed, was asleep. It was 3:15.

TWENTY-TWO

Sam's call found Philippe dozing in his white van, and he couldn't keep the yawn out of his voice when he answered.

"Rise and shine," said Sam. "Time to come to work. Don't forget to switch off your lights before you turn into the drive." He could hear the clatter of the engine being started, and Philippe clearing his throat. When he replied, his voice was doing its best to sound alert and efficient. "Three minutes, *mon général.* I'll bring the corkscrew. Over and out."

Sam grinned and shook his head. Once this was all over, he'd look around for an antique military medal — one of Napoléon's best — that he could pin on Philippe's chest for services above and beyond the call of duty. He'd earned it. And he'd probably wear the damn thing.

Sam walked across the driveway and took up his position in the shadow of Empress

Eugénie's statue. Behind him was the vast sleeping bulk of the Palais, unlit except for the glimmer of two porch lights; ahead, the gates rose in silhouette against the lights of the empty boulevard. With a silent apology to Empress Eugénie for his forward behavior, he felt beneath her flowing marble robes until his hand found the button that young Dominique had used to operate the gates. He pressed it as he heard the sound of an engine laboring up the hill, and saw the gates swing slowly open. *Merci, madame.*

Philippe kept his eye on the pinprick of Sam's flashlight and pulled up next to the pile of cartons stacked outside the cellar door. He was dressed for the evening's expedition in black from head to toe — a portly Ninja, complete with a close-fitting wool hood of the kind much in vogue with terrorists and bank robbers.

"I checked," he whispered with an air of satisfaction. "It's OK. I wasn't followed."

While they were loading the cartons, Sam suggested as tactfully as he could that the hood might attract the wrong kind of attention on the open road. Philippe did his best to hide his disappointment, and took it off before getting into the driver's seat. He peered through the windshield toward the boulevard. "*Merde!* The gates are shut."

265

"Automatic timer," said Sam. "Pick me up by the statue."

They rolled slowly through the gates, Philippe turned on the lights, and the van wheezed along deserted streets, following the signs that would lead them out of Marseille and on to the *autoroute.*

Sam collapsed in his seat, feeling drugged by an overwhelming sense of relief. The serious part of the job was over. Tying up the loose ends was going to be fun. "Have you spoken to Sophie? Is she OK?"

"I would say *très* OK. She called me late last night. She and Vial had drinks at the hotel and then Vial took her to dinner at Le Petit Nice, the hotel up on the Corniche. The chef there has just been given his third Michelin star — they say he's a magician with fish. I must pay him a visit. Anyway, she said she had a great time. I think she likes Vial very much. I told her I'd call during the night if there was a problem, or in the morning if everything had gone well." Philippe slowed down at the entrance to the *autoroute* to take a ticket from the toll machine. They were heading north, and they had the wide ribbon of road to themselves. "She's a good girl, Sophie. A little bossy from time to time, but a good girl. I didn't really know her before this — you know how it is with cousins. Even though they're family, you only see them at weddings and funerals, with everybody on their best behavior. It must be the same in America, *non?*"

But there was no answer from Sam. Sprawled in his seat, his head lolling, his arms hugging his chest, he was starting to make up for two sleepless nights. Philippe drove on in silence, his mind busy with thoughts of his scoop and the pleasant prospect of a trip to Los Angeles to interview Danny Roth. The idea of California fascinated him, as it did so many Frenchmen. Surfers, Hells Angels, square tomatoes, whales, wildfires, mudslides, Big Sur, San Francisco, Hollywood — anything could happen in a place like that. Why, they even had a European governor.

He turned off the *autoroute* at Aix and followed the smaller roads that led to Rognes and across the Durance River into the Luberon. It had been some time since he'd made this trip, and he was struck by how empty and quiet the countryside seemed after the crowds and tumult he was used to in Marseille, and how dark the darkness was. He passed the villages of Cadenet and Lourmarin, both fast asleep, and entered the narrow corkscrew road that would take them through the mountain and over to the north side of the Luberon. The steep, rocky slopes of the mountain came down so close to the nearside edge of the road that it was like driving through a jagged, twisting tunnel. And here it was darker still. It could have been a million miles from anywhere; not a place to break down. Sam snored gently through it all.

He was shaken from sleep when the van turned onto the deeply rutted dirt track that led to the old house. Philippe cut the engine but left the headlights on. He had parked facing the remains of a well, now a tumbledown circular wall of stones supporting a lopsided framework of iron, with a chain hanging from the rusty crossbar. After several unsuccessful tries, accompanied by head-scratching and curses, he finally found the stone concealing the venerable six-inch key to the front door of the house.

Sam followed him inside, where there were more curses while Philippe looked among festoons of cobwebs for the fuse box and the main power switch. With a grunt of triumph, he turned on the electricity, which produced a dribble of light coming from a forty-watt bulb hanging from the ceiling.

"*Voilà!* Welcome to the family château." He wiped a strand of cobweb from his nose and clapped Sam on the shoulder. "You slept well?"

"Like a baby." In fact, Sam felt surprisingly fresh after his nap: clearheaded and cheerful, as he always was when a job had gone well. He followed Philippe through a series of small, low-ceilinged rooms carpeted with dust, empty except for the odd ramshackle chair or table pushed into a corner.

"What happened to the furniture?"

Philippe had come to a stop in what had once been a kitchen, now stripped of anything useful. A bird's nest had fallen down the chimney and into the hearth of the stone fireplace. Propped on the mantelpiece was a faded, stained calendar from the Cavaillon fire department, dated 1995. "Ah, the furniture," Philippe said. "There were one or two really nice pieces. But the minute the old lady was in her coffin, the relatives came with a truck and cleaned the place out. I'm surprised they left the lightbulbs. They're probably still arguing about who gets what. But at least they couldn't take the cellar." He pushed open a low door in the corner and reached for the light switch, causing whatever it was in the cellar to scurry back to its hole. "We'll have to put rat poison down, or they'll eat the labels off the bottles. I think it's the old glue they like."

As in the rest of the house, the cellar had been subjected to the acquisitive attentions of the relatives, and not a single bottle remained. After the vast magnificence of Reboul's cellar, it seemed decidedly humble. A short flight of steep stairs led to the storage facilities, which were no more than shelves made from old planks resting on iron bars driven into the walls. The surface of the walls was black with mold, and the coating of gravel on the floor had worn thin, exposing patches of beaten earth. But, as Philippe pointed out, it was cool, it was humid, and it was the last place in the world one would expect to find three million dollars' worth of wine.

Bringing the cartons in from the van was a slow business, made awkward by doorways and ceilings which had been designed, it seemed to Sam, for dwarves. Were people that much shorter and smaller two hundred years ago? By the time the last carton had been put in place, both men had skinned their knuckles against the rough stone edges of the narrow doorways, and their backs ached from stooping. They had hardly noticed that while they'd been working a new day had arrived.

"What do you think?" said Philippe. "I'm not a country boy, but this is special." They were standing outside the house, looking east, where the first splinter of sunlight had just appeared above the horizon. Sam made a slow, 360-degree turn. There was no other house in sight. They were surrounded by fields that would turn purple later in the year, the clumps of lavender looking like rows of green hedgehogs. Behind them was the mass of the Luberon, misty blue in the early light.

"You know what?" said Sam. "It'll look even better after we've had breakfast. I haven't eaten since lunch yesterday."

They drove down to Apt, found a café with a terrace in the sun, and raided a nearby bakery for croissants. Big, thick-rimmed cups of *café crème* were set in front of them. Sam closed his eyes and sniffed the fragrant steam. Only in France did it smell like this; it must have something to do with French milk.

"Well, my friend," he said, "we have a rich, full morning ahead of us." Philippe, his mouth busy with croissant, raised an eyebrow. "First, we'd better check out of that hotel before Vial discovers that he's suddenly five hundred bottles short, and we need to find someplace else to stay — not in Marseille. So I'm going to need to rent a car. Then we have to find some unmarked cartons, come back to Grandma's house, repack the wine, and get rid of the other cartons. After that, we can celebrate." He checked the time and reached for his phone. "Do you think Sophie will be awake yet?"

She was. Not only that, she had anticipated a swift exit from the hotel and had already packed. She went up even further in Sam's estimation.

Philippe dropped him outside the Hertz office at the airport. He told Sam to meet him in the parking area at the entrance to the *autoroute* and went off in search of wine cartons. A friend of a friend was a *vigneron.* He would have a barn full of cartons, Philippe was sure.

In his rented Renault, Sam joined the early-morning traffic going into Marseille. He had forgotten that inside every self-respecting Frenchman lurks the soul of a Formula One driver, and he found himself in the middle of an amateur Grand Prix — tiny cars hurtling along, wheels barely touching the ground, the occupants conducting animated phone conversations while smoking and, if there was a hand free, steering. When he arrived intact at the hotel he offered up a silent prayer of thanks to the patron saint of foreign drivers, and went to find Sophie.

She was finishing breakfast, looking remarkably relaxed for someone who had just conspired in the execution of a crime. "*Alors?* How did it go?"

"Great. I'll tell you in the car. Let me get my bag and pay the bill, and then We'll take a drive. You're not going to believe this place."

By 8:30, well before Vial's working day started at the Palais du Pharo, they were on their way out of Marseille.

TWENTY-THREE

It was turning into one of those spring days that Provence does so well: not too hot, a sky of flawless, endless blue, the fields speckled scarlet with poppies, and the black skeletons of the vines softened by a green blur of new leaves. The atmosphere in Sam's rented Renault, as it followed Philippe's van through the countryside, was as lighthearted as the weather. The job was done.

"Now you can go back to Bordeaux," said Sam, "and get married to Arnaud, and live happily ever after. When's the wedding?"

"We're thinking about August, at the château."

"Do I get an invite?"

"Would you come?"

"Of course I would. I've never been to a French wedding. Any plans for the honeymoon? I could show you a good time in L.A."

Sophie laughed. "What about you? What

are you going to do next?"

"Finish up here. Then I guess I'll go to Paris to brief the people in the Knox office."

"Are you sure about that? What are you going to tell them?"

"Well, I certainly don't want to confuse them with the facts. So I thought I'd stick to Philippe's story. You know, the anonymous tip-off, the fearless reporter following up the clues that lead him back to Roth. The people at Knox won't ask too many questions once they know they're not going to have to pay out three million bucks."

Ahead of them, Philippe's van was wheezing around the final steep hairpin bend in the mountain road that led up to the plateau and the old house. Sam was looking forward to seeing him when he came to L.A. to interview Roth. They could rent a World War II jeep, hit the army surplus stores, and maybe take in one of those testaments to red-blooded virility, a gun show. It would be interesting to hear a French-man's logic applied to the question of why Americans think it necessary to have a semi-automatic assault rifle to hunt squirrels.

For the second time that morning, Philippe led the way through the house to the cellar, a large canister of raticide under one arm, a stack of cartons, folded flat, under the other. With three of them sharing the work, it took no more than an hour to repack the bottles. When the others had left the cellar, Philippe scattered a generous coating of lethal pellets on the floor, wishing the rats *bon appétit* before closing the door behind him.

He joined Sophie and Sam outside as they were loading the last of the empty Reboul cartons into the van. These would be left in a garbage dump on the way back to Marseille.

"That's about it," Sam said to Philippe. "All we need to do now is find somewhere for Sophie and me to stay tonight. Any ideas?"

Philippe scratched his head, dislodging some more cobweb. "You might be spotted in Marseille, so that's out, and you don't want to stay anywhere around here. It's too remote, and you'd be noticed. Why not try Aix? I've heard the Villa Gallici is a nice place."

And so it proved to be — small, charming, and a two-minute walk from the cafés and other delights of the Cours Mirabeau. But Sam was starting to flag. The adrenaline rush had been replaced by a pervasive, numbing fatigue. Apart from a short nap in the van, he'd been two nights without sleep. He made his excuses to Sophie, went up to his room, and toppled onto his bed fully dressed.

Six hours and a shower later, he felt sufficiently restored to venture out onto the shady terrace of the hotel and wake himself up with a glass of champagne. He turned on his phone and checked it for messages: Elena, wanting a progress report, and Axel Schroeder, fishing again. He decided to save Elena for later, and called Schroeder.

"Axel, it's Sam."

"Dear boy, I was beginning to worry about you. I hope you haven't been working too hard." He sounded like a doctor practicing his bedside manner.

"You know how it is, Axel. Scratching a living from the parched earth. But I've had a stroke of luck."

There was no reply from Schroeder. It wasn't necessary. His curiosity was almost audible.

"I found the wine. All of it."

"Where is it?"

"Safe."

Schroeder took his time to reply. "Sam, we need to talk. I happen to know a couple of people who would be very, very interested."

"I'm sure you do."

"No risk, and we could split the proceeds."

"Axel, you set it up, didn't you?"

"Sixty-forty, in your favor. A nice piece of change."

"Maybe next time, you old scoundrel."

Schroeder chuckled. "Worth a try, dear boy. You know where to reach me if you change your mind. Don't do anything I wouldn't do."

Sam looked out across the terrace. Tables had been set for dinner, and he felt a powerful urge for a steak, rare and bloody, and a bottle of good red wine. He'd call Sophie and ask her to join him. But first, Elena.

After congratulating him, she wanted to know all the details.

"Elena, it's not something I want to talk about on the phone. How soon can you get over here?"

"Forget it, Sam. That's why Knox has a French office full of French people. They do France. How soon can you be in Paris?"

"I'm planning to be there sometime tomorrow evening."

"At the Montalembert?"

"Yes. At the Montalembert. Elena . . ."

But she was all brisk and businesslike. "I'll arrange for someone from Knox to contact you there. Great job, Sam. Well done. Roth doesn't deserve it, but my CEO will be a happy guy. I'm going to tell him right now."

The call had left Sam feeling flat, and another glass of champagne did little to lift his spirits. The terrace was beginning to fill up with hotel guests and one or two flirtatious couples from Aix. Everyone seemed to be having a wonderful time, which made Sam feel flatter still. Sophie wasn't answering her phone, and the prospect of eating alone, usually something he enjoyed, held no attraction for him tonight. But there was nothing else for it. And so he spent the evening with his steak, his wine, and his thoughts.

When he met Sophie for breakfast the next morning, she explained why she'd been out of touch. Assuming that Sam would sleep through the night, she had gone to see one of those poignant, emotionally exhausting films so beloved by French directors. It had made her weep buckets, always a good sign. She had enjoyed it enormously.

"And so today," she said, "Philippe has suggested a farewell lunch before we go to the airport. He knows a little place on the port at Cassis where they do a correct *bouillabaisse*. It's not too far — less than an hour's drive. Does that sound good for you?"

It did. After a long night's sleep, Sam's disposition was improving by the minute, and it was helped even more by his first sight of Cassis. A village on the sea is a magical sight on a sunny day; a village on the sea with twelve excellent vineyards in its back garden is enough to make a man want to throw away his passport and stay forever.

Philippe was already installed on the terrace at Nino, a restaurant with the thoughtful addition of three guest rooms, in case lunch should be followed by an irresistible desire to have a siesta. Although it was still early, the terrace overlooking the port was almost full, reflecting an uncharacteristic regard for punctuality. For the most part, the Provençal might be relaxed, even cavalier about timekeeping, but his appetite is not; the stomach must be served at noon. When he looked around, Sam could see napkins already being tucked into shirt collars as menus were studied and the relative merits of a *gigot* of monkfish or a grilled *daurade* were pondered in between sips of the chilled local wine. A serious business, lunch.

"I thought we might celebrate with a glass of champagne," said Philippe, "but this is not the place to drink champagne. Here, one must drink a village wine." He plucked a bottle from the ice bucket at his side and displayed the label. "Domaine du Paternel. A treasure." He poured the wine and raised his glass. "To our next meeting, wherever that may be. Today, Cassis. Tomorrow" — with a wink and a waggle of the eyebrows directed at Sam — "Los Angeles?"

The lunch was long and convivial and the *bouillabaisse* superb, but despite the lure of a siesta upstairs they managed to get to the airport with time enough to have a final coffee. Their few days together had been, as Philippe said, *vraiment chanu,* the best possible time, which he assured the others was high praise indeed coming from a native of Marseille. And so, with much garlic-scented kissing and embracing and promises to meet up in Bordeaux for Sophie's wedding, they went their separate ways: Sophie to Bordeaux, Sam to Paris, and Philippe back to working on his scoop. He already had the first part written in his head: the tip-off, the discovery of the wine in its remote hiding place, and the realization that he had stumbled onto a treasure trove. The options to develop the story after that were many and fascinating. Philippe could see a very entertaining few weeks ahead of him.

From his window seat, Sam took one final

look at the Mediterranean as the plane turned its back on the sun and headed north. For once, he was less than exhilarated at the thought of going to Paris. Despite its occasional patches of squalor, he had found Marseille to be a fascinating and very engaging city, a city of enormous character. It had a tough charm that appealed to him, and the people were good-natured and friendly. How far Marseille's lurid reputation was from its reality.

Cloud cover settled in over central France, and the plane landed in a monochrome Paris, layers of gray superimposed on layers of gray from ground to sky. It was strange to think that the sharp, crystalline light of Provence was only an hour away. The Marseillais would be leaving work about now, gathering on café terraces for *apéritifs* and gossip while they watched the sun go down. Philippe would be bent over his notes in one of the little bars he used as an office. As Sam's taxi swerved and sprinted its way down the Boulevard Raspail toward the hotel, he felt an early twinge of nostalgia.

He dropped his suitcase on the bed and hung up his jacket. A quick shower would take away the rumpled feeling he always had after a plane trip, and he was halfway out of his trousers when the room phone rang. He hopped across on one leg to answer it.

"So tell me — what does a girl have to do to get a drink in this place?"

His heart jumped at the sound of her voice. "Elena? It's you? You're here?"

"Who else were you expecting?"

Standing there, a broad smile on his face, his pants around his ankles, he was the happiest man in Paris.

Twenty-Four

The other inhabitants of the Chateau Marmont had either already gone to work or were still in bed. Sam had the pool to himself. He'd completed his daily self-appointed task of twenty laps, and now stood dripping in the morning sun.

Life was good, he thought, as he toweled his hair dry. He and Elena had finally given up sparring with each other and were moving cautiously and pleasurably toward some form of commitment. He looked forward to introducing her to Philippe, who was going to be in town the following week to interview the man he called Monsieur "Rot." (No matter how well he spoke English, he shared with many of his countrymen a difficulty when it came to pronouncing *th*.) And there were one or two interesting possibilities on the horizon. All he needed to make the morning perfect was coffee.

He pulled on his bathrobe and made his way through the barbered, glossy jungle that separates the pool from the main hotel building, stopping at the front desk to pick up a copy of the *L.A. Times.*

"Mr. Levitt?" It was one of the affable young men behind the desk. "We've been calling your apartment. You have a visitor. A gentleman. We put him at your table in the corner."

Bookman again, Sam thought. He often dropped by for breakfast when he was in the neighborhood. Looking for clues, he always said. Sam strolled across the garden, glancing at the day's headlines as he went. When he looked up from the paper, a half smile already on his face, he stopped as though he'd walked into a wall.

Smiling back, nodding, immaculate in a putty-colored linen suit, Francis Reboul got to his feet and extended his hand.

"I hope you don't mind my dropping in like this," Reboul said as he sat down and gestured for Sam to do the same. "I took the liberty of ordering coffee for us." He poured for both of them. "There's nothing like that first cup after a swim, is there?"

Sam, feeling at a distinct sartorial disadvantage, was struggling to get over his surprise. He looked across at the neighboring tables, checking for large men in dark suits.

Reboul had read his mind, and was shaking his head. "No bodyguards," he said. "I thought it would be more comfortable with just the two of us." He sat back in his chair, completely at ease, his eyes bright with amusement in his mahogany face. "How fortunate that I kept the card you gave me. As I recall, you were in the publishing business the last time we met." He dipped a sugar cube in his coffee and sucked it thoughtfully. "But somehow I feel that literature might be a little tame for a man with your rather special talents. I wouldn't be surprised to hear that you've made a career move. Would it be indiscreet of me to ask what you're doing now?"

Sam hesitated for a moment. He was rarely at a loss for words, but Reboul had him completely off balance. "Well," he said. "The book business is pretty slow right now, so I'm sort of resting between assignments."

"Excellent," said Reboul. He seemed genuinely pleased. "If you're not too busy, I have a proposition that might interest you. But first you must tell me something, just *entre nous*." He leaned forward, both elbows on the table, his chin resting on his clasped hands, his expression intent. "How did you do it?"